A.R. SGROI

Our Thing: Part I

Blood and Empire

EMPIRE
QUILL PRESS

Our Thing

PART I
Blood and Empire

A.R. SGROI

"In a city carved by ambition and stained with blood, one man dared to claim a future that was never promised to him."

I

ACT I

Blood and Opportunity

1

Ellis Island, Iron Hearts

Part I - 1924 - New York City

The fog rolled in thick off the Hudson, wrapping the docks in a shroud that clung to every crate, lamppost, and rusted nail like a ghost that refused to pass on. Salvatore Vitali stepped off the boat in silence, his leather shoes touching American soil for the first time. The scent of saltwater, coal smoke, and sweat hit him all at once. It smelled like work. Like struggle. Like something he could own.

He carried no suitcase—just a worn coat over his shoulders and a letter from a man named Carlo Mancini folded three times in his inner breast pocket. The coat was his father's. The letter was an offer. The rest, he would take for himself.

Behind him, the RMS *Carmania* loomed like a fading memory. A vessel of second chances for some, escape for others. For Salvatore, it was a coffin. Sicily was dead to him. Burned behind the eyes by blood debts and a vendetta he didn't lose—he simply survived.

' "Hey, paisano!" a voice barked in thick Brooklyn Italian. Salvatore turned.

A boy—no older than fifteen—ran up to him, smudged with coal and grinning like the devil. "You Salvatore Vitali?"

Salvatore nodded.

The boy handed him a newspaper folded into quarters. Hidden inside: a small envelope with an address scrawled in precise ink. "You ain't supposed to open it here. Carlo don't like eyes."

Salvatore took the paper, slid the envelope into his pocket, and offered the boy a coin. The kid was gone before it hit his hand.

He stood for a long moment at the edge of the pier, staring out over a city brimming with motion. Trucks groaned. Laborers shouted in four different languages. The skyline was sharp and uneven, growing by the hour. New York was loud—arrogant, even. But beneath all that noise, Salvatore could feel it: the rhythm. The pulse.

Cities have bones, he remembered his uncle once telling him. *And every bone can be broken if you know where to strike.*

He turned from the river and walked toward the city.

The address led him to Red Hook, Brooklyn—a neighborhood thick with Sicilian tongues, where the smell of tomato and diesel drifted from stoops and alleyways. The tenement was five stories tall, sagging like a tired boxer. A brass number plate on the door: 212-A.

He knocked twice. A slit opened in the door. No words— just a single eye inspecting him like a butcher grades beef. The eye vanished, the door opened.

Inside was dark wood, sharp cigars, and quiet menace.

Three men sat at a poker table, their coats draped on the backs of their chairs like wolves shedding skins. At the center sat Carlo Mancini.

He rose slowly, tall and broad-shouldered, dressed in the kind of pinstripe suit that came with bloodstains in the lining.

"So," Mancini said, lighting a cigarette with a gold lighter. "The butcher of Partinico lives."

Salvatore's jaw twitched, but he said nothing. He knew better than to take bait, even when it came wrapped in compliments and poison.

"I heard what you did to the Capuano brothers before you left Sicily," Mancini continued. "That kind of reputation follows you. But reputation don't feed you here, Signore Vitali. Work does. Loyalty does."

"I didn't come to chase ghosts," Salvatore replied. "I came to build something."

Mancini smiled, smoke curling between his teeth. "Good. Because ghosts are cheap in New York. It's the living that cost you."

That night, Salvatore took a cot in a two-room flat above a butcher shop. The walls were thin. He could hear arguments through plaster, the rhythm of footsteps upstairs, the low hum of the city's restless breath. He stared at the ceiling for a long time, replaying every word Carlo Mancini had said.

You want work? There's whiskey coming in through the docks from Montreal. You'll help with the unload. Quiet work. Dangerous, if you're stupid. Profitable, if you're not.

He knew what it meant—a test.

And he wouldn't fail.

Beneath his mattress, he slid a small photo. It was black and white, worn at the corners. A younger Salvatore stood beside a man with cold eyes and a sharper mustache—his father. Behind them: a vineyard that no longer existed. Burned. Buried.

He didn't look at the photo long. Memory was a weight, and New York demanded speed.

Tomorrow, he would begin.

And if this city truly had bones?

He would break them—one at a time.

The next morning was soaked in cold mist and sweat at the Brooklyn Docks. Salvatore arrived early—too early. A thin film of fog hung over the East River, broken only by the shifting silhouettes of dockworkers hauling crates, shouting in coarse accents, cursing the weight of barrels filled with Montreal whiskey.

He kept his mouth shut and his eyes open.

"Hey, Siciliano!" someone barked from behind a stack of crates. A wiry man with a crooked nose waved him over. "You're Carlo's pick? You don't look like much."

"Neither do you," Salvatore answered without hesitation.

The man froze. Then—unexpectedly—laughed. "You got stones, I'll give you that. Name's Nico. You keep pace with me, maybe I don't tell the foreman you're just here to get shot."

They moved fast, hands wrapped in canvas gloves, unloading barrels from a disguised fish truck marked "Caputo's Seafood." Every third barrel was labeled incorrectly—those held the good stuff: uncut rye smuggled through Canada by bribes and luck.

Salvatore noted everything: the rhythm of the lifts, the men watching from the shadows, the badge of the beat cop who walked by and deliberately looked away. He noticed how Nico flinched at sudden sounds and how the man in the trench coat across the street tapped a rhythm on his leg that didn't match the pace of the others.

He was being watched.

Tested.

As the last barrel rolled into the alley's false storage door, a truck pulled up. Four men jumped out fast—no uniforms, no questions, just guns and rage.

"Drop it!" one shouted in a Bronx accent.

For a heartbeat, everyone froze.

Salvatore didn't.

He hurled a crowbar across the alley, catching one of the gunmen in the side of the head. Chaos erupted. Nico pulled a pistol from his boot. Two shots rang out. One of the newcomers screamed.

Salvatore dove behind a barrel, ripped the lid from another, and hurled a bottle like a Molotov—glass shattered, liquor sprayed, and in the panic, he tackled the second gunman to the ground, slamming his head once—twice—into the cobblestones.

By the time it was over, two men were down. One bleeding badly. The others ran.

"You crazy bastard," Nico muttered, catching his breath. "You want to get killed on your first week?"

Salvatore stood slowly, knuckles bloodied. "If it's the wrong week, then maybe I shouldn't wait."

Nico looked at him again—this time with something closer to respect.

Part II - Midday – Mancini's Club, Back Office

Carlo Mancini didn't speak for a full minute after Nico finished recounting the story. He leaned back in his leather chair, polishing a silver ring with his thumb.

"You disarmed two men," Carlo said at last. "With bottles and guts."

Salvatore shrugged. "It wasn't planned. They were sloppy."

"No. You were prepared."

Carlo stood and walked to the window overlooking Fulton Street. "In this city, Salvatore, you don't win by killing fast. You win by knowing who dies slow. You think with that same instinct, that same fire, you'll go far."

He turned.

"But you don't work for me yet. You earn that."

Salvatore met his gaze. "Then give me something harder."

Carlo smiled like a man who loved burning bridges just to watch the glow.

"You'll meet Aldo Rossi tonight. He handles Harlem distribution. Doesn't like new blood. See if you can convince him otherwise. Without bullets, preferably."

That night at a club in East Harlem, Aldo Rossi looked like a man built from smoke and hard words. He wore a suit that cost more than the entire block, and the pistol beneath it had likely taken a dozen lives.

He didn't shake hands.

"Carlo's dog," he said by way of greeting. "You bite, or just bark?"

Salvatore sat across from him. "I'm here to clean your mess, not add to it."

Aldo's eyes narrowed. "You know what your family name means up north? Blood. Vendetta. Old-country baggage."

Salvatore didn't flinch. "In Sicily, we cleaned our own streets. We can do the same here."

Aldo grunted. "We'll see."

He tossed Salvatore a small key. "There's a shipment coming in Thursday. Problem is, Mancini didn't clear it with the boys uptown. Cops might hit it. Or worse—Mancini's competition. You make sure it lands. Clean. Quiet."

Salvatore stood. "And if it doesn't?"

Aldo's smile didn't reach his eyes. "Then maybe you go back to Sicily. Or somewhere colder."

Part III - Thursday, 2:03 A.M. — Harlem Freight Yard

The train yard was quiet—too quiet for a city that never really slept. Salvatore crouched between two crates, watching the old switch house across the yard. He'd memorized the schedule from the foreman's notes. The liquor was coming in via freight disguised as refrigeration equipment, stored in insulated canisters to throw off suspicion.

Only one thing could go wrong: people.

Chris, one of Aldo's men, had been assigned to "assist." Salvatore didn't trust him. The guy talked too much, didn't blink enough, and kept his coat buttoned even when the cold broke.

"Relax," Chris whispered from beside him. "You're acting like this is your first job."

"It's the first one that matters," Salvatore replied.

He spotted the train headlights approaching from the east. Right on time. But as the boxcar hissed to a stop, two things happened in quick succession: first, the freight operator climbed down and gave the signal to unload. Second, a figure moved in the shadows near the south gate—one not listed in the manifest.

Not one of ours.

Salvatore signaled Chris to stay down and quietly moved around the stack of steel drums. From the shadows, he saw them—three men in long coats, walking like wolves. Not cops. Professionals.

The kind you didn't bribe. The kind who weren't there to steal.

They were there to send a message.

The first gunshot cracked like thunder through the yard. The guards scattered. Chris panicked—returned fire and hit nothing. Salvatore acted instead of thinking. He dashed across open gravel, dodged a falling crate, and tackled one of the attackers as he reloaded.

They hit the ground hard. Salvatore's elbow crushed the man's nose. He grabbed the pistol and fired once—quick and clean.

The second man disappeared into the yard.

The third, however, had taken cover near the engine. Salvatore crept through shadows and steam. When he struck, it was without hesitation—two shots to the chest before the man could raise his weapon.

Silence returned—but it wasn't victory.

Chris was gone.

Salvatore found him near the north exit. Shot in the leg,

bleeding, but breathing.

"You—you crazy bastard," Chris stammered. "You went at them like you didn't care."

"I cared," Salvatore said, hauling him up. "That's why we're alive."

Later that morning, Aldo Rossi sipped espresso while reading a folded paper.

"Three dead," he said, without looking up. "None of them cops. And the liquor?"

"Safe," Salvatore replied.

Aldo set the paper down and studied him. "You think you passed the test."

Salvatore didn't answer.

Aldo smirked. "You didn't. Because it wasn't about killing. It was about keeping your head. You did both."

He tapped his fingers on the desk. "You're not like the rest of them. You don't chase respect. You build it."

Salvatore nodded once. "Then let me build something bigger."

Aldo leaned back and let the silence grow long between them.

"You get one crew. Your pick. You report to Carlo, but you work Harlem with me. You screw this up, there won't be a second chance."

Salvatore extended his hand. "I won't."

Aldo stared for a moment longer, then shook it.

Salvatore stood on a rooftop overlooking Brooklyn. The city pulsed below him—a storm of ambition, greed, and motion. Smoke curled from chimneys, cars choked narrow streets, and somewhere far off, a siren wailed into the dark.

He reached into his coat and unfolded the old photo again.

His father's face stared back—cold and stoic. A reminder of where he came from. But not where he was going.

Salvatore lit a match and let the flame reach the photo's edge.

The fire licked across the paper, curling it into black ash.

"I'm not here to inherit," he muttered.

"I'm here to take."

2

The Streets of Red Hook

Part I - Summer, 1924 - Brooklyn

The summer heat clung to the bricks like a second layer of mortar, thick and oppressive, pressing down on Red Hook with a weight that made tempers short and deals shorter. But Salvatore Vitali thrived in pressure. Pressure made cracks. Cracks let you in.

By July, he had carved out a modest stretch of influence— quiet, invisible to most, but unmistakable to the men who mattered. Carlo Mancini had put him to work running liquor routes through Brooklyn's dockyards and speakeasies, and Salvatore obeyed the surface of that order. He ran what he was told to run. He paid who he was told to pay.

But underneath, he was building something else entirely.

Not an empire. Not yet. A network.

He started with the immigrants. Sicilians, mostly. Men who had crossed the ocean chasing bread and safety, and instead found themselves elbow-deep in backbreaking labor for crooked foremen and Irish cops who used their nightsticks like punctuation marks. These men didn't trust anyone, but they understood fear. And they respected action.

So Salvatore gave them both.

When the butcher on Court Street was robbed and the police shrugged, Salvatore returned the stolen goods himself, then left the thief hanging by his heels from a fire escape.

When the landlord of a tenement raised rents by twenty percent overnight, Salvatore sent three men to "renegotiate" the lease terms. The next week, the building had free heat and rent forgiveness for two months.

He never took a fee. Not yet.

Instead, he took memory.

He took names.

He took notes.

Salvatore's base of operations remained a half-renovated tenement above an abandoned laundromat on Sullivan Street. A wooden sign reading *FOR LEASE* still hung from a cracked window, giving the illusion of disuse. Inside, the rooms had been gutted and refitted with oil lamps, ledgers, crates of bonded whiskey, and a map of Brooklyn with dozens of thumbtacks, all connected by red thread.

Rico Navarro stood beside him that morning, his sleeves rolled up, sweat darkening the edges of his collar. He had a notebook in one hand and a growing sense of awe in the other.

"You're running this like a bank and a militia," he muttered. "Every time I think I know what you're doing, you're doing five things more."

"That's the point," Salvatore replied. "Mancini has soldiers. He wants noise. I want structure."

"You're not worried he'll think you're moving too fast?"

Salvatore turned toward him, calm and exact.

"If he doesn't see it, he's blind. If he does and lets me, I'm useful. If he sees it and tries to stop me…"

He let the sentence trail off.

Rico nodded. "Got it."

That afternoon, Salvatore attended a card game in the back room of *Giglio's Tailor Shop*—a legitimate front where half the chairs were filled with men who'd broken more laws than they could name, and the other half were pretending they hadn't.

Among them was Franco Bellandi, a mid-level fixer for the Lombardis. He wore cream suits, chewed mint leaves instead of smoking, and had a habit of giving compliments that sounded like insults.

"You're climbing fast, Vitali," Franco said as he shuffled. "Mancini sends you into Brooklyn, and now half of Red Hook's offering you espresso like you're the mayor."

"People appreciate being listened to," Salvatore replied, checking his cards without expression.

Franco smirked. "Careful. Loyalty's a currency that gets devalued real quick around here."

Salvatore looked at him evenly. "Only when the banker is dishonest."

The table fell quiet for a moment before someone laughed nervously and changed the subject.

But Salvatore knew Franco's warning wasn't just clever chatter. The Lombardis were watching him now. Everyone was.

That evening, Salvatore walked the streets of Red Hook with

the confidence of someone who didn't need to announce his presence. The heat hadn't broken. The air felt like the inside of an oven, and the sound of arguing couples, barking dogs, and distant radios filled the night.

As he passed the alley behind Giancarlo's bakery, a small voice called out.

"Signore Vitali!"

A boy—maybe ten—ran up to him barefoot, his hand clutching a folded scrap of paper. "Mama says thank you for the potatoes. She says… she says it meant a lot."

Salvatore knelt, took the paper, and gave the boy a silver coin. "Tell your mother she owes me nothing. But tell your uncle he should stop playing dice in Mancini's territory. It's not safe."

The boy nodded solemnly and disappeared into the dark.

The note was short and unsigned, but Salvatore recognized the handwriting: Rosa's.

You haven't changed, except now your kindness is dangerous. Don't forget who's watching.

Part II - Two Days Later - Carlo Mancini's Social Club

The smell of polished wood and cigar smoke filled the room like a second skin. Salvatore sat in a stiff-backed leather chair opposite Carlo Mancini, who leaned on his cane with one hand and stirred his coffee with the other. No one else spoke while Carlo thought.

"You've been busy," Mancini said finally, not looking up. "Too busy for a man I've barely given orders to."

Salvatore didn't blink. "You said I had leeway."

"I did. But you're treating leeway like it's a leash, and you're walking it around the whole neighborhood."

Salvatore let the accusation hang before replying. "I don't take territory. I earn trust. And I make you money. Quietly."

Mancini studied him. "And the loyalty? That yours or mine?"

Salvatore met his gaze, unwavering. "That depends. Are you going to make me choose?"

Carlo exhaled slowly. The two men stared across that space between them—not as boss and subordinate, but as predators measuring the size of each other's bite.

Then Carlo smiled. "You remind me of myself twenty years ago."

"I hope not," Salvatore replied. "I plan to last longer."

Later that night at the Red Hook dock house, Rico Navarro locked the side entrance behind them. Salvatore stood over a table littered with maps, invoices, shipping manifests—all sourced from whisper networks and informants in three boroughs.

"We've confirmed it," Rico said. "That shipment last week was hijacked by someone in Mancini's own crew. Frankie Scalese. He's been skimming crates, selling to the Irish uptown."

Salvatore frowned. "You sure?"

"As sure as the guy who confessed it while bleeding out in my bathtub."

Salvatore tapped his knuckles on the table. "And Carlo doesn't know?"

"He doesn't—or he doesn't care. Either way, we do."

They were at a crossroads. To expose Scalese would earn favor, but also draw attention. The kind of attention Salvatore wasn't ready for. Not yet.

"Not yet," he murmured aloud.

"What?" Rico asked.

"We watch. Let Scalese dig deeper. When we move, we move with proof. And witnesses."

Rico grinned. "You're cold."

"No," Salvatore said. "I'm building something that won't fall apart when I blink."

The Red Hook Church had a Sicilian immigrant meeting the next day. The smell of basil, old wood, and fresh bread mingled as a dozen Sicilian elders sat at folding tables, passing wine and news between them. Salvatore arrived unannounced but welcomed.

These were the old men who once pulled fishing nets by hand, who wore their pride like armor and kept their pain under their tongues. Salvatore listened more than he spoke— he always did here.

"Signore Vitali," one of them said between sips of bitter red wine, "you helped my son find work at the pier. That boy was ready to leave the city before you."

Salvatore nodded, respectful. "We take care of our own. That's the only way we stay standing."

Another man, toothless and sharp-eyed, leaned forward. "You act like a don, but you say you're not one."

"I'm a man who remembers where we came from," Salvatore said. "And I want to make sure we don't go back there."

They murmured approval—not obedience, but something close. Salvatore didn't need their fear. He needed their belief.

And that night, when he returned to his flat, he found an envelope slid beneath his door—no name, no seal, just one word in perfect, sharp cursive: Careful.

Meanwhile at a restaurant in Upper Manhattan in a darkened booth lit only by candlelight, Aldo Rossi sipped bourbon and watched Carlo Mancini's consigliere whisper into his ear. Aldo was a man who rarely reacted, but tonight he raised one graying eyebrow.

"He's got his own books?" Aldo asked.

"Yes," the consigliere said. "Separate ledgers. Same product, different entry. And he's paying his boys more than Carlo does."

Aldo looked out the window, watching the cars glide by like sharks in the fog.

"Vitali's building an army," he said.

"No," the consigliere replied. "He's building a future."

Aldo finished his drink.

"We'll see how long he keeps it."

Part III - Two Weeks Later - Sullivan Street Flat

The map on Salvatore's wall had changed.

What once looked like a chessboard of neutral zones and dangerous patches now bled with fresh markings—red thumbtacks for loyalty, black for threats, and blue for those he had yet to read. In two months, he had connected fourteen business owners, three dock crews, five foremen, and nearly a dozen street-level operatives to his growing network.

Not one of them had sworn loyalty with blood or rings. They simply owed him.

Favor by favor. Problem by problem. It was the old Sicilian way, layered into the new American mold.

Rico entered the room, pulling a cigarette from behind his ear. "Frankie Scalese is making another drop tonight. Same back lot in Gowanus. This time with two of his own men instead of Mancini's. He's pushing hard."

Salvatore nodded. "We move tonight. Quiet. No blood."

Rico blinked. "You're going to let him walk?"

Salvatore looked at him calmly. "I'm going to let him confess."

Frankie Scalese never saw the trap coming that night at the Gowanus Warehouse, just before midnight.

When he stepped into the warehouse office to count the shipment receipts, he found himself locked in—alone—with Salvatore sitting across the table, legs crossed, sleeves rolled to his forearms.

"I always wondered how much whiskey fits into a man's pride," Salvatore said. "Seems you've been measuring."

Frankie's face went pale. "Look, it's not what—"

"It's exactly what it looks like," Salvatore cut in. "You stole from Mancini. You sold to outsiders. And you lied about both."

Frankie looked around, as if expecting to be beaten—or worse. But no one moved. No one even breathed.

Salvatore opened a drawer and pulled out a pad and pencil. "You're going to talk. Clearly. Calmly. Then you're going to walk out of here and deliver that letter to Carlo Mancini yourself."

Frankie blinked. "You serious?"

"You've got two options, Frankie. Walk out as a man begging forgiveness—or leave in a crate labeled 'apples.' Your call."

Frankie swallowed. He chose the letter.

The next day, Carlo Mancini's face didn't change as he read the letter. But the hand holding his coffee twitched once—barely.

When it ended, he set it down and looked at Salvatore.

"You did this clean. No blood. No headlines."

"I gave you loyalty," Salvatore said. "And proof."

Mancini leaned back. "I should be afraid of you."

"You should be proud."

The silence between them was heavy, but not hostile.

"You want a seat at the table, don't you?" Mancini asked.

"No," Salvatore said. "I want my own table. In your house. For now."

Carlo chuckled softly. "For now."

On Sunday, Salvatore waited on the stone steps after mass, the collar of his jacket turned up against the late-summer wind. Rosa exited with her mother, her arm linked gently through the older woman's. Her eyes flicked to him, deliberate. Measured.

She walked straight past, but as she passed, she spoke just loud enough for him to hear.

"You'll make it, Salvatore. Just don't forget who you had to step on to get there."

He didn't turn. Didn't speak.

He just watched her go.

Later that night at Salvatore's Sullivan Street flat, the light from the oil lamp cast flickering shadows across the map.

Salvatore stood alone, glass of wine in hand, eyes tracing the paths between streets, names, debts, dangers. He had built something in two months that some men couldn't manage in ten years. Not an empire—not yet—but the bones of one. And bones could grow.

Or they could break.

He wasn't sure which he was building yet.

He only knew he wouldn't stop.

3

The Wedding Pact

Part I - Autumn, 1924 - Brooklyn

The wedding was not grand. It was not meant to be.

There were no cathedral bells, no marching bands, no press clippings or mafiosi parades in open-top cars. Salvatore Vitali wouldn't allow it. Nor would Rosa. Their marriage was held in the basement of St. Anthony's Parish—the same church where they once lit candles for lost relatives and whispered prayers that felt more like apologies.

There were thirty-seven guests. No more, no less. Every one of them chosen by Salvatore or Rosa with the precision of a general assembling his war council.

The pews were worn, the altar was plain, and the priest spoke in a hushed, firm voice that had once consoled widows of men Salvatore himself had watched disappear.

Rosa wore a simple ivory dress with lace trim. Her veil was hand-stitched, borrowed from her late grandmother. Her hair was braided in a crown that shimmered only when the candlelight caught it just right. She looked not like a bride, but like a sovereign taking the mantle of a crownless kingdom.

Salvatore wore black. Not a tuxedo—black wool, black tie, black shoes polished to a mirror. He looked like a man who knew mourning better than celebration, but today, he made an exception.

They did not speak their vows loudly. They barely looked at the priest. They looked only at each other.

And when the moment came, *you may kiss the bride*—Salvatore did not hesitate. He kissed her slowly, like a man sealing a pact he had once feared would never be made.

The reception was held two blocks away, in the back garden of a boarding house owned by Rosa's cousin, where the food was Sicilian, the wine was red, and the music came from an accordion older than half the guests.

There were toasts.

Rico Navarro said nothing sentimental but gifted the couple a ledger of their growing business operations, wrapped in white ribbon. "Build something with this," he said. "Not just the books. The future."

Carlo Mancini didn't attend. But he sent a bottle of imported grappa with a note: *Loyalty is love that pays interest. Congratulations.* Signed simply: "C."

Rosa's mother, widowed and severe, watched the evening with eyes sharp as ice picks. She spoke only once, to Rosa, quietly:

"Be careful, figlia. Men who build empires rarely leave room for wives."

Rosa's smile was practiced. "Then I'll take the corners."

Later, when the sun had long set and the guests had begun to drift home—some laughing, some staggering, a few making backroom deals over slices of almond cake—Salvatore and Rosa stood in the alley behind the house.

She smoked a cigarette with one hand and held his with the other.

"I thought you didn't smoke anymore," he said.

"I thought you didn't marry women who could outthink you," she replied, exhaling through a grin.

He looked at her sideways. "I don't think I ever had much of a choice."

"No," she said. "You didn't."

They stood there a long while, neither saying what they were both thinking—that this marriage wasn't just love. It was strategy. It was armor.

And maybe, just maybe, it was a kind of salvation neither of them believed in but both needed anyway.

When they returned to the flat—his flat, now theirs—Rosa removed her veil and hung it over the back of a chair. She walked to the window, pulled the curtains aside, and stared out over the Brooklyn streets, lit orange by distant gaslights and the occasional flicker of a passing car.

Salvatore poured two glasses of wine.

"Do you regret it?" he asked, offering her one.

She took the glass. "Regret is for people who had better options."

"You had better options."

"I had different ones," she corrected.

He stepped beside her. The city stretched before them like a map of broken promises waiting to be rewritten.

"We're a strange pair," he said.

"No," she said. "We're the only kind that survives in this world."

They clinked glasses. And drank.

Outside, somewhere in the distance, a car backfired—sharp, loud, and sudden.

Neither of them flinched.

Part II - One Week Later - Red Hook

It didn't take long for the marriage to change things.

Not just the domestic rhythms, though Rosa's presence had quietly transformed the Sullivan Street flat into something closer to a sanctuary, filled with quiet music, fresh bread, and books stacked in corners Salvatore never used. No, the real changes came from the way people looked at him now.

A married man wasn't just a man. In the circles Salvatore moved in, he was a statement. He was grounded. Permanent. Intentional. He wasn't just building power anymore—he was building legacy.

And everyone noticed.

The first sign came from Franco Bellandi, the Lombardi fixer with the mint-leaf habit. He arrived at the Sullivan Street flat two days after the wedding, uninvited but not unwelcome. He brought a gift—an antique gold pen—and an invitation.

"A wedding gift," he said, setting the box gently on the table. "And a conversation."

Salvatore raised an eyebrow. "I don't remember inviting you."

"That's the thing about power, Vitali," Franco said smoothly. "You don't need to be invited. You just need to arrive before the door closes."

Salvatore gestured to the seat. "Talk."

Franco didn't waste time. "You've grown fast. Carlo sees it. The rest of us feel it. But now—now you've got a wife. A partner. That changes things."

"Only if you think she's a liability."

Franco's smile thinned. "On the contrary. Rosa is a chess move. One that tells the board you plan to play to the end."

He leaned forward.

"So now the question is, whose side are you playing from?"

That evening, Salvatore told Rosa about the visit while she grated cheese over a pot of pasta.

"He doesn't trust you," she said without turning. "He's trying to figure out whether I'm your tether or your trigger."

"You're neither," Salvatore replied.

"I'm both," she corrected. "And that's what makes me useful."

He watched her for a moment. "You don't mind being used?"

She turned to face him, hand still holding the grater. "Only if I'm not also using you."

There was no smile. No malice. Just understanding. Deep and mutual.

Meanwhile, Rico Navarro was busy.

Salvatore had given him a new task: identify which of the existing Mancini capos were loyal only to the paycheck, not the man. Rico compiled a list of six names. Two were obvious. One was a stretch. Three were dangerous.

"They're watching you," Rico said one night in the flat,

pacing while Salvatore poured wine. "Not Mancini. These guys. Soldiers, lieutenants. The ones who think your marriage means you're soft."

"I'm not."

"I know that. You know that. But they see the pasta on the table, the books on the shelves. They think you're domesticated."

Salvatore sipped the wine. "Then let them try to break in."

The test came on a Wednesday.

Salvatore's crew had just finalized a deal to move crates of bonded rye through a meat-packing warehouse in Carroll Gardens—legit on the surface, but a perfect cover for the real product. One of Mancini's capos—Vittorio Scali, a boar of a man who never shaved and never shut up—showed up at the loading dock unannounced with three of his own men.

"This is our turf now," Scali declared. "New orders from up top."

"There are no new orders," Rico shot back.

Scali grinned. "Maybe not on paper. But things change when boys start playing house. Thought maybe we'd relieve the pressure on our newlyweds."

Salvatore stepped out of the shadows.

"No need," he said calmly. "My wife handles pressure better than most of you handle a spoon."

Scali's grin faded. "Careful, Vitali."

Salvatore nodded to the truck. "Take one crate. For your trouble. But tell your crew this—next time they come without an invite, I'll send them home in pieces."

Scali didn't reply. He just left with the crate. And a message.

The retaliation came fast.

Two nights later, a storefront in Vinegar Hill—run by one of Salvatore's earliest allies—was torched. No casualties, but the message was clear: you're not untouchable.

Rico wanted to strike back. Hard. Now.

But Salvatore said no.

"We wait," he said. "We set a trap. A public one."

Rosa, listening from the table, looked up from her notebook. "You're planning to humiliate them."

"I'm planning to remind them I'm not the one who changed," Salvatore said. "They did. They got lazy. I didn't."

The plan unfolded over four days.

Salvatore leaked word—through backchannels, barbers, and butcher shops—that a high-value shipment would be moving through Dumbo under light guard. He made sure Scali's people would hear it.

Then he waited.

When the ambush came, Salvatore's real crew—hidden in the rafters of the warehouse—cut the lights, sealed the exits, and caught them with their hands on the crates.

No bullets. No blood.

Just photos.

Photos that made their way into the hands of Carlo Mancini.

Photos that proved Scali's crew was undermining internal routes, freelancing, disrespecting the chain of command.

Carlo summoned Scali the next day.

He returned with one hand in a sling and no position to speak of.

Salvatore never mentioned it.

He didn't need to.

Rosa found a letter slid under their door. No name. No return address.

Inside: one sentence, scrawled in ink.

She's the reason they'll come for you.

Salvatore read it. Folded it. Burned it over the stove.

"I thought we were past letters," Rosa said, arms crossed.

"They're getting scared," Salvatore said.

"Good," she replied. "Scared people make mistakes."

He met her gaze. "So do married men."

She touched his cheek. "Then we'll make ours together."

Part III - Late Autumn, 1924 - Brooklyn

The first cold winds of fall swept down from the harbor, biting into Red Hook like an early warning. Leaves rattled in gutters. The streets turned quieter. People walked faster, heads down, coats tight. Even the docks—normally alive with shouting, sweat, and motion—seemed to move slower under the weight of approaching winter.

But Salvatore Vitali moved like the season didn't touch him.

In the span of weeks, he had consolidated more ground than any capo under Mancini's banner. The smuggling routes through Carroll Gardens were secure. Two more foremen at the docks had quietly pledged allegiance. And most importantly, the attacks had stopped.

Not because the enemy gave up.

Because the enemy was regrouping.

One evening, Salvatore stood on the fire escape outside the

Sullivan Street flat, smoking alone, watching a horse-drawn cart carry barrels of flour toward the tenements.

Rico joined him, hands in his pockets, eyes narrowed.

"We've been too quiet," Rico said. "I don't like it."

"Quiet is good," Salvatore said.

"Not when it comes from people like Mancini. Or the Lombardis. Or Aldo Rossi, for that matter."

Salvatore exhaled smoke. "They're watching. Testing. Seeing if the wedding was a show or a strategy."

Rico glanced back toward the window, where Rosa moved through the kitchen, setting down plates.

"They're wondering what she is to you."

"She's mine."

"That's not what I mean."

Salvatore didn't reply. He didn't need to. The truth sat between them like a coiled wire—too tight to touch, too dangerous to ignore.

That night, Salvatore and Rosa dined with Father Leone, the priest who had married them.

He was a middle-aged age man with warm eyes and a strong jaw—one of the few who treated Salvatore like something other than a threat or a meal ticket.

They ate lamb and olives in the rectory's small parlor. Talk drifted between Scripture, politics, and the neighborhood's gossip. But Salvatore knew the visit wasn't for pleasantries.

Father Leone sipped wine and set the glass down gently.

"There's talk," he said, "that your name is being spoken with respect—and fear."

Salvatore didn't deny it.

The priest continued. "You remember what I said at your

wedding?"

"You said God sees all covenants," Salvatore replied.

"I said love is a fire. Warm in its light. Destructive when left unchecked."

Rosa tilted her head. "You think we're destructive?"

"I think power is," the priest said. "And people drawn to it often mistake warmth for safety."

Salvatore stood, placing his napkin on the table. "I appreciate the sermon, Father. But Rosa and I don't mistake anything. We see clearly."

The priest nodded once. "Then I'll pray your clarity outlives your enemies."

Three nights later, the first real test arrived.

A messenger from Aldo Rossi—a tall, pale man in a fedora two sizes too large—knocked at the flat at midnight. Rosa answered the door, her robe belted neatly, a knife in her hand behind the frame.

Salvatore took the message at the threshold.

No words. Just a small velvet pouch.

Inside: a woman's earring.

Salvatore's face didn't change, but his hands tensed around the fabric.

He recognized it.

It belonged to Isabella Ferranti, a local business owner who had hosted a meeting of Sicilian shopkeepers on Salvatore's behalf the week before.

The message was clear: *you're not untouchable—and neither are those who believe in you.*

The next day, Salvatore walked alone into Rossi's lounge on

the East Side.

The room quieted when he entered.

Aldo Rossi sat in a leather booth in the back, flanked by two men. He didn't rise.

"Vitali," he said. "Didn't expect you."

"Then you've forgotten who I am."

Aldo smiled faintly. "I remember. You're the mouthy one with an attitude problem who likes to push his luck. Makes you dangerous. Or stupid."

Salvatore sat across from him. "You sent a message. I'm answering it."

Russo poured himself a drink. "You're building fast, kid. I don't like fast. Fast doesn't ask permission."

"I didn't know I needed it."

"You always do. Whether you ask or not."

Salvatore leaned in. "Then let's speak plainly. You touch another one of mine—anyone who owes me, respects me, or breaks bread with me—and I won't come to your lounge next time."

Rossi's smile vanished. "And what? You'll send soldiers?"

"No," Salvatore said. "I'll send architects."

Aldo frowned. "What the hell does that mean?"

Salvatore stood. "It means I won't tear your house down. I'll build one taller. Next to yours. And I'll make sure no one remembers you ever had one."

He left without waiting for a reply.

That night, back in the flat, Rosa handed him a small box.

"A gift?" he asked.

"No. A favor."

Inside: a ring. Old. Heavy. Not gold—iron, etched with a

Latin phrase he couldn't place.

"Where did you get this?"

"My grandfather," she said. "He wore it during the war. And when he traded horses after it."

Salvatore turned it over. "What does it say?"

Rosa met his eyes. *"Fidem ferro fundavi."*

He didn't speak Latin.

"I founded my loyalty in iron," she translated.

Salvatore slipped the ring on.

It fit.

Salvatore and Rosa stood together in silence on the rooftop that night, wind tugging at her coat, the skyline glittering like a knife's edge across the river.

"Do you regret it?" he asked her again.

"Regret is for the weak," she said.

"Then what do you fear?"

She hesitated, just for a breath.

"Being remembered for the wrong reasons."

Salvatore didn't laugh. He didn't reassure her.

Instead, he nodded.

"You won't be."

4

Whiskey & War Paint

Part I - Winter, 1924 - Brooklyn Waterfront

The waterfronts didn't belong to anyone—not really.

They were warzones dressed in fog, dotted with rusted cranes, grease-stained warehouses, and a carousel of bribes that spun faster than the ferries. You could rent protection. You could buy silence. But own it? No. The water didn't care who had the muscle. It only respected who moved faster—and who hit first.

Salvatore Vitali understood that.

That winter, he moved from local muscle to something sharper. Bootlegging wasn't new, but how you played the game was everything. Most crews paid off the cops, bribed a few customs clerks, and prayed no one else undercut them.

Salvatore had a better idea.

He stole.

Not from the innocent. Not from neighbors. From rival crews—Irish, Lombardi, even a few outfits up from Jersey who thought Brooklyn was just a refueling stop. He watched their drop spots, tracked their trucks, learned their weaknesses. And then he hit them, hard and silent, like a ghost with calloused hands.

It started with Pier 13.

Word came from one of Rico's sources that a shipment of Canadian rye meant for the Delaney crew would arrive by fishing boat, lightly guarded, with a delayed pickup crew.

A mistake.

Salvatore's men—Rico, Gio Ferrara, and a pair of new faces called Luca and Mirko—struck at midnight. No guns. Just blades, crowbars, and muffled boots on wet gravel.

The job took eleven minutes.

When the Delaney crew arrived an hour later, all they found was a bent loading ramp and a smear of oil across the dock.

The rye? Gone.

The rumor? "Some ghost outfit cleaned it out."

Salvatore made sure no one corrected the story.

By February, the Vitali crew had hit six separate operations— each time faster, smarter, cleaner. Their stolen stockpile was stored in the lower levels of a meat packing plant Salvatore had acquired under Rosa's name.

The irony amused him.

"Everyone's worried about me being soft," he told her one night, walking the icy floor between stacked barrels of whiskey and crates of Scotch. "But you've got more liquor in your name than half of Manhattan."

She smirked. "Maybe I'll start a speakeasy. Call it *The Don's Wife.*"

He grinned. "Only if you let me play piano."

"You play piano?"

"I don't," he said. "But that's never stopped me before."

Rico handled distribution. Quietly. He didn't flood the streets. He funneled product through existing networks and made new ones where he had to—bartenders, corner clubs, jazz parlors, even an upscale supper club in Midtown that never asked questions and always paid in cash.

But the most valuable connection came from Luther Clay, a former railroad worker turned black-market logistics genius who operated out of Bed-Stuy.

Luther was sharp, sober, and absolutely amoral when it came to business. He didn't care about family names. He cared about percentages.

"You give me product," Luther said at their first meeting, "I'll give you a city's worth of thirsty bastards who don't give a damn where it came from—as long as it's wet and hot."

Salvatore extended a hand. "Then let's get them drunk."

By spring, Salvatore had a full operation in motion: stolen liquor, clean logistics, a stable of quiet drivers, and distribution that stretched from Staten Island up through Harlem.

And the rivals noticed.

First came the warnings—graffiti, slashed tires, missing crates.

Then came the beatings. One of Luther's drivers turned up in a gutter, teeth scattered like dice. Still breathing. Barely.

Rico wanted blood.

"Delaney's crew hit us," he said. "It's retaliation. We should burn their dock."

But Salvatore shook his head. "Too loud. We're still shadows. We stay shadows."

Instead, he arranged a meeting with a twist.

He invited Seamus Delaney himself to a back room in a Crown Heights boxing gym. No threats. No pretense.

Just whiskey.

Delaney arrived with two men and a limp from an old bullet wound.

"I should kill you," he said after the first pour.

"You should," Salvatore agreed. "But you won't."

"Why not?"

"Because I'm not your enemy," Salvatore said. "I'm your lesson. You got sloppy. You stopped watching the boats. You paid the wrong cops. That's not my fault. That's yours."

Delaney stared at him.

"And now?"

"Now I offer you something better. You sell my liquor at your prices. No overhead. No risk. I even give you credit for it."

"You're out of your mind."

Salvatore leaned back. "Maybe. But I'm making a lot of money being crazy."

Delaney laughed. And poured another glass.

Part II - Spring, 1925 - Brooklyn and Beyond

With Delaney on board—or at least pacified—Salvatore's bootlegging network grew from a chain into a web. Liquor moved in refrigerated fish trucks, hollowed-out flour crates, and through funeral processions with caskets full of rye instead of bodies. Nothing was sacred. Everything was possible.

Luther Clay expanded the operation into Jersey City, even testing deliveries through train yard bribes. Harlem speakeasies began carrying "Vitali Scotch"—a name Salvatore hated but allowed, knowing that branding was power. It gave the liquor identity. And it gave him leverage.

But the more people drank, the more people asked questions.

And questions were dangerous.

Rico Navarro was the first to say it out loud.

"You're not a thief anymore," he said, spreading ledgers across the butcher block table in the back room of the Sullivan Street flat. "You're an operator. Which means the families are going to want a cut—or a funeral."

"They're already getting a cut," Salvatore said.

"Not enough. And not official."

Salvatore's face stayed calm, but the pause said enough.

Rico leaned forward. "We're too big to stay quiet. You want to keep this? You need recognition. Or a war."

Salvatore hated both.

The first shot wasn't a bullet. It was a demand.

Marco Lombardi, youngest son of the Lombardi patriarch, sent word through a nightclub singer: a sit-down. Neutral ground. No bodyguards. Just two men.

Salvatore chose a hotel lounge in Manhattan—a soft-lit, white-glove place where men spoke in code and women pretended not to hear.

Marco arrived wearing silk and sarcasm. He didn't shake hands.

"You've been busy," he said, taking a seat. "Some say bold. Others say suicidal."

Salvatore raised an eyebrow. "Depends on the audience."

Marco smiled, thin and sharp. "My father doesn't like surprises."

"Then he shouldn't close his eyes."

Silence. A waiter brought whiskey. Neither drank.

Salvatore broke the stillness. "I heard you were taking over for your father."

Marco smiled again. "Functionally, yes. Formally not yet."

Marco leaned forward, and a note of seriousness fell between them.

"You're making money that used to be ours," Marco said. "That makes you interesting. And dangerous. And potentially valuable."

Salvatore nodded. "Go on."

"Join us. Be a partner, not a parasite. You give us twenty percent of your operations, and we give you protection, legitimacy, and access."

"And if I say no?"

Marco leaned in. "Then the streets start talking in gunfire. And you know how quickly memories get buried in this city."

Salvatore didn't answer. He just stood, buttoned his coat, and left a folded $100 bill beneath the untouched glass.

When he returned to the car, Rosa was waiting in the back seat.

"How was it?" she asked.

"Predictable."

That night, Rosa lit a cigarette and leaned against the bedroom window. Below, the city throbbed—lights, car horns, stray laughter from a nearby alley.

"You're going to say no, aren't you?" she asked.

"I already did."

"You realize what that means."

"Yes."

She turned toward him. "Then you need to move first."

Salvatore nodded slowly.

"Tomorrow," he said. "We stop stealing."

Rosa frowned. "And start what?"

"Controlling."

The next day, Salvatore met with Luther Clay and Rico in the meatpacking warehouse. He spread out a list of names—twelve venues across the city, all of them operating off Vitali supply.

"These are ours now," Salvatore said. "Officially. No more 'partners.' No more 'borrowed shelves.' We buy in. Or buy out."

Luther grinned. "You want to own them?"

"Not all of them. But enough to set the message."

Rico crossed his arms. "And what message is that?"

Salvatore looked at both men.

"We're not pirates anymore. We're a fleet."

The first acquisition was Clemente's Tavern, a rundown jazz bar in Bed-Stuy that owed three months' rent and half its inventory to a dead Irishman. Salvatore sent Gio Ferrara with a contract and a bag of cash. The owner signed before the offer was finished.

The second was tougher—Eden, a speakeasy in Midtown run by a slippery woman named Claudia Voss who wore diamonds like armor and carried a Derringer in her garter.

She demanded triple.

Salvatore paid double.

She signed anyway.

But the third location never signed.

The Yellow Room, a basement joint in Hell's Kitchen, was run by a Lombardi cousin named Dino Spada. The second he got word of the offer, he trashed the delivery truck and beat one of the drivers bloody.

No more diplomacy.

That night, Salvatore walked into the Yellow Room with Rico, Gio, and a man named Massimo who spoke five languages and broke noses in all of them.

They didn't talk.

They emptied the place in under ten minutes—patrons out, bartender paid off, and Dino left handcuffed to his own radiator with a note pinned to his chest:

"Your cousin makes offers. I make decisions." – S.V."

The retaliation came two days later.

A storefront owned by Luther Clay's cousin exploded just after dawn. No deaths, but the warning was loud.

Rico wanted war. Again.

"We need to answer," he said. "They're not going to stop."

Salvatore said nothing. He stood in the doorway of the bombed-out building, smoke curling in the morning air, the scent of sulfur and burnt wood clinging to his coat.

"I'm not going to answer," he said. "I'm going to finish the conversation."

"How?"

Salvatore stared at the wreckage.

"We hit something they don't think we'll touch."

Part III - One Week Later - Hell's Kitchen

The Vitalis didn't hit a liquor warehouse.

They hit a payroll drop.

It belonged to the Lombardis, moved every Friday morning from a Midtown butcher shop to a private bank through a laundry service. Two armed men, one unmarked car, and a clerk who didn't ask questions.

Salvatore changed the question.

At 7:14 a.m., the Vitali crew intercepted the drop at a stoplight. They didn't fire a shot. Massimo posed as a beat cop, flagged the car, and when the doors opened, Gio and Luca stepped in fast and quiet. The guards were stripped, bound, and blindfolded. The clerk was left untouched, told to count to 300 before moving.

By the time the Lombardis knew what happened, Salvatore had half a week's pay for three neighborhoods sitting in a vault beneath the Sullivan Street flat.

It wasn't about the money.

It was about the message.

We can take what we want. And we can leave you breathing.

The next night, Salvatore met with Carlo Mancini.

It was their first face-to-face in a month.

Carlo sat behind his heavy oak desk, cigar lit, a newspaper folded next to his glass of amaro. He didn't look angry. He looked amused.

"You're making me popular," he said. "The Lombardis are knocking on my door every other hour. The Russos are sniffing around your routes. And the DeMarcos? They're just waiting for someone to bleed."

Salvatore stood across from him, calm.

"I haven't crossed any lines."

"You've made new ones."

Carlo tapped ash into a crystal tray.

"Do you want to be a boss, Salvatore?"

"No."

"Then what?"

"A future. One that doesn't belong to men too old to change."

Carlo studied him.

Then he leaned back, smiling.

"I'll give you a pass. One time. Because I like what you're building. But make no mistake—if the city turns against you, I won't catch you. I'll bury you."

Salvatore nodded. "I wouldn't expect anything less."

Back at the Sullivan Street flat, Rosa was waiting. She sat on the couch with a book in her lap, half-read, her mind elsewhere. She closed it when he entered.

"Well?" she asked.

"He let it go," Salvatore said.

"For now?"

"For now."

She walked to the window. "And what about the next line you cross?"

"I'm not crossing lines anymore," Salvatore said.

"I'm drawing them."

Rosa looked back at him.

"You realize the more power you gain, the closer you move to the edge."

Salvatore stepped behind her, wrapping his arms around her waist.

"Then it's a good thing I married someone who sees cliffs before I do."

That weekend, they hosted a private dinner for key allies—Rico, Luther, Gio, Massimo, and Claudia Voss from Eden. A dozen names who had helped grow the Vitali bootlegging empire from stolen crates to its own underground kingdom.

The dinner wasn't just celebration.

It was loyalty.

And Salvatore made it clear.

"We're not thieves anymore," he said, raising his glass. "We're merchants. We move product better than anyone in this city. We don't ask permission. And we don't beg forgiveness."

He looked at each of them.

"But we remember. Who helped. Who risked. Who bled."

He raised his glass higher.

"To legacy. And to those who build it."

Glasses clinked. Wine flowed. For a night, they were untouchable.

But across the city, in a shadowed brownstone in Tribeca, Marco Lombardi sat with two of his father's top enforcers.

He lit a cigarette, exhaled slowly, and unfolded a map of Brooklyn.

"Vitali thinks he's a king," Marco said. "Let's remind him what happens to kings who steal crowns."

5

Five Families, One City

Part I - May, 1925 - Midtown Manhattan, The Astoria Club

The Astoria Club was a fortress dressed in velvet.

Built in the 1880s for bankers and industrialists, its chandeliers weighed more than most men, and its columns rose like the backs of titans. It was the kind of place where power didn't just gather—it crystallized.

That morning, five cars arrived in silence and sequence, dropping off men who didn't speak their names and didn't need to. They wore dark coats and heavy expressions. Their footsteps didn't echo, but the air shifted as they moved.

The summit had been called.

Five families. One table.

And for the first time, Salvatore Vitali had been invited to sit.

Carlo Mancini led the way in, flanked by his consigliere and two bodyguards. He looked tired but sharp, like an old blade you didn't realize could still cut until it bled you.

Behind him came Marco Lombardi, radiant with youth and contempt, his silk gloves pristine, his smile empty.

Then Antonio Russo, whose raspy breath carried more weight than his words ever had. He nodded to no one. He simply sat.

The DeMarco contingent arrived last—three men and no Don. Rumor said Vincent DeMarco hadn't left his Long Island estate in months. Some said he was ill. Others said dead. Either way, his chair was empty.

And that, Salvatore noted, was the most dangerous thing in the room.

He entered without ceremony.

No entourage. No display. Just Rico Navarro walking two paces behind, coat unbuttoned, eyes scanning. Salvatore wore a dark three-piece, crisp white shirt, no tie. A statement in itself—formal, but not bound.

The other men stopped talking when he approached the round table. Twelve feet across, dark mahogany, inlaid with a brass compass rose. Symbolic, once. Now ironic—none of them had a direction anymore.

"Vitali," Carlo said, nodding. "Glad you came."

Salvatore took his seat.

"I didn't come for ceremony," he said. "I came to listen."

The meeting began with pleasantries. Each man spoke in half-truths, complimenting growth, raising toasts to peace, and swearing—without saying it—that the city was big enough for them all.

It was all lies.

The alcohol was real, though. So was the tension.

"I think we all know why we're here," Marco Lombardi said after the second round of drinks. "Things have shifted. Routes have changed. Product moves faster through Brooklyn now than through the Bronx. That's good for some."

Salvatore didn't blink. "You're welcome."

Marco smiled coldly. "We all want stability. No one wants another war."

"Then stop losing yours," Rico muttered.

Carlo raised a hand. "Enough. We're not here to throw stones."

Antonio Russo coughed into a handkerchief, then spoke hoarsely. "We need order. The city's growing. Feds are sniffing. We need to clean up. Tighten ranks. And maybe…"

He let the sentence hang.

"…reconsider leadership."

There it was.

Salvatore said nothing. He watched the others.

Marco leaned forward. "The Families need a chair again."

"A boss of bosses?" Carlo asked.

"Not in name," Marco said. "In function. Someone to coordinate. Set terms. Balance."

Salvatore's eyes drifted across the table to DeMarco's empty seat.

"Interesting timing," he said.

During a break, Salvatore stepped out onto the club's second-floor balcony. The city below stretched out in steam and stone, oblivious to the chessboard above.

Rico lit a cigarette behind him.

"They want someone to take the chair," Rico said. "But none of them wants the risk."

Salvatore nodded. "Because the moment someone sits, every other man starts sharpening knives."

"And yet," Rico said, "you're the only one not afraid of it."

"I'm not afraid of it," Salvatore said. "Because I'm not here to sit. I'm here to see."

"See what?"

He looked back at the room inside, where four families pretended unity.

"The cracks."

Inside, the summit resumed.

Carlo raised the issue of port access—specifically, the dock crews in Bay Ridge. Mancini-controlled, but increasingly "influenced" by Russo cash.

Antonio waved it off. "We don't want turf. Just smoother operations."

"And who defines smooth?" Salvatore asked. "You skim the crates, delay my shipments, pay off my men—and call that smooth?"

Antonio didn't answer. But Marco did.

"You're playing above your weight, Vitali. This summit is a courtesy."

"No," Salvatore said. "It's a mistake."

The table went quiet.

Salvatore leaned forward, voice low and measured.

"You all think power is about chairs and votes. But the men in this city don't follow orders anymore. They follow efficiency. Product. Paydays."

He pointed toward the empty chair.

"That seat? That's the past. And it's still bleeding."

Carlo ended the session soon after.

He didn't declare a decision. No one did.

But Salvatore saw what he needed to see.

DeMarco's absence wasn't illness. It was decline. Vincent DeMarco was the closest thing the Families had to a boss of bosses, and now they had no leadership. They were vulnerable and splintered. And the others—so busy posturing—they didn't realize the vacuum was already forming.

In silence. In shadow.

Waiting to be filled.

Part II - Three Days Later - Sullivan Street Flat

The rain hadn't stopped in two days. Outside, Brooklyn blurred under a curtain of gray, water slipping through gutters, soaking into cracks that had long forgotten dryness. Salvatore stood by the window, watching the city weep while Rosa read aloud from the morning's paper.

"'DeMarco Family Denies Rumors of Illness—Leadership Remains Intact,'" she read. "You believe it?"

"No," Salvatore said. "They wouldn't bother lying unless it was true."

She folded the paper and set it down.

"They're covering for weakness. Someone's moving behind the scenes."

"Probably someone inside the DeMarco circle."

Rosa arched an eyebrow. "Or someone outside it. Someone

watching the walls fall from the other side."

Salvatore didn't reply. He didn't need to.

She already knew he was considering it.

That afternoon, Rico Navarro met with two former DeMarco enforcers in the back room of Rossi's Barbershop, an unofficial hub of quiet men with violent hands. Over black coffee and sandwiches, they laid out their frustrations.

"Vincent's got his nephew running things now," said one. "Nico DeMarco. Kid's useless. More interested in girls and gin than balance sheets."

"Whole thing's coming apart," said the other. "We ain't had a sit-down with a real number man in a month. No drops. No pay bumps. Just whispers."

Rico listened. He nodded at the right moments. Then he offered something simple:

"A better way."

He didn't name Vitali.

He didn't have to.

That night, Salvatore reviewed the list: nine names in the DeMarco periphery who had value—men with muscle, knowledge, or loyalty for sale. None were high-ranking. But that was the point. High ranks stood out. Shadows moved in silence.

"Start with Rocco Filieri," Salvatore told Rico. "He runs the warehouses in Flushing. Quiet man. Smart. Overlooked."

"And if he won't flip?"

Salvatore smiled. "We won't ask him to."

Two days later, at the Flushing Docks, Rocco Filieri returned

from his night rounds to find his office cleaned. Not robbed—
cleaned. Papers stacked. Desk polished. Inventory ledgers
corrected. And on his desk, a bottle of 15-year rye with a note
beneath it.

"We see you. Let us know when you're ready to be seen." – S.V.

Rocco didn't mention it to his boss. He didn't tear up the
note.

He just poured a glass, sat back, and considered how long it
had been since anyone noticed he existed.

Meanwhile, Marco Lombardi wasn't sitting idle.

The summit had rattled him. Not because of Salvatore's rise,
but because the others hadn't stopped it. Mancini was aging.
Russo was coughing himself into irrelevance. DeMarco was a
ghost.

Marco saw the future standing across from him at that table.
And it had *Salvatore's* face.

He summoned his consigliere, Emilio Parelli.

"We need a crack," Marco said. "Something we can use."

"Blackmail?"

"Too early."

Parelli tapped a finger on a file. "There's a woman. Rosa
Vitali. Born Rosa Licata. Her brother's name used to come up
in arms smuggling before the war. Went missing in Palermo.
You want that dug up?"

Marco shook his head. "No. Not yet. We don't smear.
We *shape.* Get me names. Anyone in his crew who's been
underpaid, overlooked, second-guessing. Everyone's loyal—
until they're not."

Back in Brooklyn, Salvatore met with Luther Clay inside a

shuttered jazz club.

The rain had kept the streets quiet, and the inside smelled of dust, bourbon, and old leather.

"I'm hearing things," Luther said. "Half the city thinks you're replacing DeMarco already."

"I haven't made a move."

"Not yet," Luther said. "But silence is a kind of move, too."

Salvatore nodded. "What do you need?"

"Protection. Your routes are bleeding into Harlem. Russo's boys are starting to watch. One of my runners took a pipe to the ribs last week."

Salvatore leaned forward. "You want soldiers?"

"No," Luther said. "I want certainty."

Salvatore smiled faintly.

"Then I'll give you both."

That evening in the backroom of the Eden Speakeasy, Claudia Voss had seen enough summits and backstabbings to know when something was about to snap. She poured Salvatore a glass of gin and leaned over the table.

"You're pushing without pushing," she said. "It's impressive. But it's not subtle anymore."

"It doesn't need to be," Salvatore replied. "The vacuum's growing."

"And you plan to fill it?"

"No," he said. "I plan to reshape the floor around it so the others fall in."

She whistled low. "You really think they'll let you?"

"I don't need permission. I need momentum."

Back at the flat, Rosa was finishing a letter when Salvatore walked in. She watched him from across the room, her eyes reading him like a ledger.

"You made a move," she said.

"No. Just a nudge."

"You're three steps ahead of yourself."

Salvatore took her hand. "Not if I know where I'm going."

She looked at him closely. "And do you?"

He didn't answer. Not with words. But outside, the city was changing.

And Salvatore Vitali was shaping it—one nudge at a time.

Part III - Two Weeks Later - Long Island, DeMarco Estate

The gates were rusting.

The ivy that once decorated the stone walls now choked them. Weeds pushed through the gravel driveway. The great house sat like a forgotten mausoleum.

Inside, the DeMarco family was dying—and Salvatore Vitali wasn't the one killing it.

It was doing that just fine on its own.

Vincent DeMarco hadn't been seen in public in six weeks. Rumors ranged from a stroke to a nervous collapse. His nephew, Nico, had assumed operations, but no one respected him. His orders contradicted each other. His cash dried up. His men began defecting.

And behind closed doors, two capos began negotiating with Salvatore.

Salvatore didn't gloat.

He didn't celebrate.

He listened.

He watched.

And he absorbed.

Piece by piece, block by block, the DeMarco structure fell into his hands without a single shot fired. Rocco Filieri in Flushing. Martino D'Angelo in Fort Greene. Two lieutenants in Vinegar Hill. The flow was slow, but steady.

"You're gutting them," Rico said one night over whiskey. "Without ever drawing blood."

"I'm offering homes to orphans," Salvatore replied.

Rico smirked. "You're adopting a whole damn family."

"Only the useful ones."

"And the rest?"

Salvatore took a long sip.

"They'll join. Or disappear."

But Marco Lombardi wasn't fooled by silence.

The Vitali rise wasn't subtle anymore.

It was *inevitable*.

He called a private meeting with Antonio Russo and Carlo Mancini in a brownstone parlor on East 88th. No soldiers. No advisors.

Just two aging giants of the old world—and one younger lion sharpening his teeth.

"He's consolidating," Marco said. "Not just DeMarco turf—people. Soldiers. Routes. Even you two are benefitting from his logistics."

Antonio shrugged. "That boy moves liquor faster than railroads. What do you want us to do—stop making money?"

Marco slammed his hand on the table. "I want you to stop pretending this doesn't end with him sitting in *that chair!*"

Carlo lit a cigar, unmoved.

"Maybe he should."

Marco stared at him.

"You'd let him rule?"

Carlo exhaled. "I'd let him stabilize."

Antonio coughed. "The boy's not stupid. But we've survived bigger storms."

"Then you're both already dead," Marco muttered.

Salvatore was ready for retaliation.

He expected a bomb. A shooting. A message soaked in blood.

Instead, he got something worse.

Silence.

The kind that meant planning.

The kind that meant fear had evolved into calculation.

At Rosa's urging, he increased security. Not visibly—no thugs on the stoop or rifles in windows. Instead, he changed routes, shifted meet points, rotated drivers, and rewired his inner circle like a maze.

"Your crew's tight," Rosa said, brushing her hair at the vanity. "But they're men. And men bleed."

"I know," Salvatore replied.

"Then start thinking like someone who wants to outlive them."

He nodded.

He was.

A week later, Claudia Voss brought news from Midtown.

"They're circling each other," she told Salvatore over gin and jazz. "Lombardi's talking to the feds. Russo's arming old allies. Mancini? He's playing both sides."

Salvatore listened.

"They're waiting for one of two things," Claudia said. "You to make a mistake—or someone else to make one first."

He looked past her to the window, where the city skyline glittered like the edge of a blade.

"Then maybe," he said, "it's time to give them one."

That Friday, a DeMarco warehouse went up in flames. The fire was swift, surgical, and devastating. No casualties. But everything inside—records, product, payroll—turned to ash. No one claimed it. No one needed to. The city whispered one name anyway.

Vitali.

Rico pulled Salvatore aside. "We didn't do it."

"I know."

"Should we correct them?"

Salvatore shook his head. "Let them believe it."

Two days later, Salvatore received a letter. Typewritten. Clean. No threats. Just two lines:

The chair is never empty for long. Watch who sits.

He didn't smile. He didn't burn it. He folded it carefully, slid it into a drawer, and poured himself a drink.

That night, he and Rosa stood on the roof, watching the lights flicker over the harbor.

"They're afraid of you now," she said.

"No," Salvatore replied. "They're afraid of losing to me."

She took his hand. "Same thing."

He said nothing.

But deep down, he wondered: If the chair wasn't empty much longer… Would he sit? Or would he be pushed?

6

Aldo's Offer

Part I - June, 1925 - Rossi Social Club, East Harlem

The room smelled of sweat, wood polish, and betrayal.

The Rossi Social Club hadn't changed in years. The same creaky floors. The same cracked window behind the bar. The same worn felt on the poker tables where fortunes had been won, lost, and buried. But now, it felt different. Hollow. Like something sacred had rotted under the varnish.

Salvatore knew the smell.

So did Aldo Rossi.

The man was already seated when Salvatore arrived. He wore a gray suit with a darker gray scowl, his thinning hair combed with precision, his eyes hidden behind gold-rimmed glasses that made him look softer than he was.

He didn't rise. He didn't offer a drink.

"Sit," Aldo said.

Salvatore did.

Rico Navarro stood behind him, silent and still. No

greetings. No pleasantries. Just the low hum of a ceiling fan and the distant knock of dice in the back room.

"You've been busy," Aldo said.

"So have you."

"I've been *watching*," Aldo corrected.

Salvatore nodded. "That's work, too."

For a long moment, nothing moved between them. Just the fan spinning overhead, slicing the air with slow, deliberate rhythm.

Then Aldo reached into his coat and pulled out a piece of paper—folded, stained, and already older than it should've been.

"This," he said, sliding it across the table, "is an import route out of Havana. Untapped. Clean. And outside everyone else's books."

Salvatore didn't touch the paper.

"I assume there's a reason you're showing it to me."

"There's always a reason."

"And a price."

Aldo's eyes narrowed. "You're sharp, Vitali. You always were. I liked that about you. Back then."

Salvatore waited.

"I'm offering you half," Aldo said. "We move through Cuba. You handle stateside logistics. I handle the ships. Fifty-fifty. Quiet. Fast. No names. No flags."

Rico shifted behind Salvatore. "You're not the quiet type anymore."

Aldo ignored him.

"If we do this," he said, "you double your distribution. You step out of the DeMarco mess. And you make more money than the rest of those tired bastards combined."

Salvatore still didn't reach for the paper.

Instead, he looked Aldo dead in the eye.

"Why me?"

Aldo didn't flinch. "Because if I don't offer it to you, someone dies. Maybe me. Maybe you. Maybe someone else. But blood gets spilled."

He leaned in.

"And I've buried enough friends this year."

Outside, the Harlem streets buzzed with afternoon heat. Vendors shouted beneath awnings. Trolleys screeched on rusted tracks. Kids chased dogs past storefronts where cigarettes were still sold in tins.

Salvatore walked in silence, Rico beside him.

"You don't trust him," Rico said.

"No."

"But you're thinking about it."

Salvatore nodded.

Rico stopped. "Sal, he's trying to rope you into something you can't walk out of."

"I know."

"Then why even consider it?"

Salvatore turned toward him, voice low.

"Because he's right. If I say no, someone dies. And I'd rather choose who."

Back at the Sullivan Street flat, Rosa was organizing files from their expanding Harlem distribution line. Maps, dates, and contacts—all alphabetized, cross-referenced, and tagged by territory.

She looked up as Salvatore entered.

"You're quiet," she said.

"I had a meeting."

"I figured. You only walk that stiff when you're thinking about something you hate."

He sat across from her.

"Aldo offered me Havana."

Her hands paused over a stack of folders.

"The docks?"

"And the rum. Straight routes. No customs. Just the Cuban ports, the East River, and a handful of quiet hands in between."

"And he wants you to be his partner?"

"Fifty-fifty."

Rosa leaned back, eyes narrowing.

"Which means he doesn't need a partner. He needs a shield."

Salvatore nodded.

"If this goes bad," she said, "you don't just lose a shipment. You lose the north shore. You lose Brooklyn's protection."

"I know."

"And if it goes right?"

He didn't answer immediately.

"If it goes right," he said, "I own something no one else touches."

Rosa stood, crossed the room, and kissed his forehead.

"Then make sure you touch it first."

That night, Salvatore sat alone with a bottle of aged rye and the unfolded Havana route spread across the table. It was elegant. Efficient. Simple.

Too simple.

He circled three points—two ports in Matanzas, one in Havana—and began checking dates against his own drop schedules.

The overlap was clear.

Someone else had been using the same ports. Quietly. Slower. Less profitably.

Probably DeMarco.

Which meant Aldo wasn't just trying to start a new route.

He was trying to *take one back.*

Salvatore smiled to himself.

"A devil's handshake," he whispered. "Dressed like a favor."

At midnight, he sent a runner to Aldo with a message:

We're in. My terms. Meeting at the cold house. No eyes. No noise.

– S.V.

Part II - Midnight - The Cold House, Red Hook Ice Depot

The Cold House wasn't a metaphor. It was an actual ice depot—abandoned, windowless, and frozen year-round. The kind of place used in the summer to store perishables and in the winter to hide corpses. Its walls were thick, its doors heavier, and its isolation near the water made it the perfect place to hold quiet conversations or make loud statements.

Salvatore arrived just after midnight, dressed in black, wool collar high against the damp salt air. Rico Navarro came with him, coat unbuttoned, cigarette already burning. No words passed between them on the walk in. They both knew what this was:

A meeting.

A negotiation.

And possibly the beginning of a war.

Aldo Rossi was already inside, sitting on a wooden crate beneath a broken lightbulb. The flicker made his face twitch with every pulse. He was alone, or at least appeared to be.

Salvatore approached calmly, gloves still on, eyes sharp.

"You got my message," he said.

"I don't miss appointments," Aldo replied.

"You've missed alliances before."

Aldo smirked. "Maybe. But I never miss money."

They stared at each other for a long moment. Then Salvatore reached into his coat and pulled out a folded document—his own version of the partnership.

No handshake.

Just paper.

"This is how it works," he said. "We split distribution—forty-sixty. You handle international intake. I manage stateside logistics. You get priority on three routes. I get exclusivity on two. We share customs leverage, warehouse space, and four front businesses. Joint expansion only by mutual agreement."

Aldo raised an eyebrow. "Forty-sixty? You think I need you that bad?"

Salvatore stepped closer. "No. I think you're already bleeding, and I'm the only tourniquet that won't snap your leg off."

Aldo laughed—loud and long, echoing in the empty space. "You got balls, Vitali."

"No," Salvatore said, "I've got leverage."

He handed the paper over.

"Take it. Or walk away and find out how many people still answer when *you* call."

Aldo read the document in silence. His eyes didn't move quickly—they moved carefully. He didn't want to miss the knife hidden in the paragraph.

Eventually, he folded the paper again and tucked it into his breast pocket.

"I'll sign," he said. "But I want one assurance."

Salvatore waited.

"If this goes bad," Aldo said, "I get the first shot. I won't be the one waiting for permission to bleed."

"You won't have to," Salvatore replied. "If this goes bad, no one bleeds. They just vanish."

Back at Sullivan Street, Rosa read the terms and underlined three sections in red ink.

"He gave you everything but access to Havana security detail," she noted. "That's where he'll keep control. That's the leash."

"I know," Salvatore said. "It's just long enough to think he's free."

Rosa looked up. "You're betting on his greed."

"I'm betting on his fear."

She circled a phrase in the document—*mutual discretion in emergency arbitration.*

"This," she said, "is your weapon."

He nodded. "If he betrays the deal, I have cause. And if I act first, it's preemptive."

"Not criminal."

"Just business."

She smiled faintly. "And what about his crew?"

Salvatore leaned back. "That's the next move."

The Rossi crew was strong on the waterfront but fractured inland. Two capos, both aging, each trying to solidify their own turf. Salvatore sent quiet feelers through Rico—small offers disguised as favors. Help with a trucking contract here. A clean bookkeeper there. Payment upgrades. Interest-free loans.

The goal wasn't to steal.

It was to soften.

To remind them that loyalty to Aldo was *tradition,* but loyalty to Vitali was *progress.*

A week into the partnership, the first joint shipment moved through Pier 17—eight crates of aged Cuban rum labeled as ceramic tile imports. Customs waved it through without a glance.

By midnight, it was already being poured into glasses in Manhattan, Brooklyn, and Harlem.

The money rolled in fast.

Too fast.

Rico counted the take with clinical precision. "We made more in one night than we used to in three weeks. And nobody pulled a trigger."

"Yet," Salvatore said.

He already knew the peace was a mask.

That Friday, Salvatore attended a sit-down with a Harlem club owner, James "Red" Tillman, who ran two dance halls and kept a finger in every liquor barrel from 125th to the Bronx. He'd recently shifted from Lombardi supply to independent sources.

Salvatore offered him a better deal: lower prices, guaranteed delivery, and security.

Red smiled over his cigar. "You play this game smart, Vitali."

"I play it like I intend to win."

Red raised his glass. "Then may the old lions keep sleeping."

But old lions don't sleep forever.

That Sunday, Salvatore received a call just after noon. One of Aldo's men—Victor Sapienza, mid-level enforcer, known drinker, and sometime leaker—had been found dead in a boarding house in Queens.

Shot twice in the chest.

No forced entry. No witnesses.

No warning.

Salvatore stood with the receiver in hand, letting the silence hum against his ear.

It had begun.

That evening, Salvatore met Aldo in a restaurant basement in Little Italy—no guards, no paperwork, just questions.

"You lose a man," Salvatore said.

Aldo's face was blank. "I lost an idiot."

"You think it was a message?"

"No," Aldo said. "I think it was a mistake."

Salvatore studied him.

"You didn't order it?"

"No."

"Then who did?"

Aldo shrugged.

"Someone who doesn't want us working together."

Salvatore narrowed his eyes.

"Or someone who doesn't want *you* working with *me*."

Part III - The Next Morning - Flushing Rail Yard

Victor Sapienza's body had been cleaned up, boxed, and buried before the sun rose. Officially, it was ruled a gambling dispute. Unofficially, no one believed that. A man like Victor didn't die over dice. He died because someone wanted silence—or chaos.

Salvatore wasn't convinced it was either.

He stood beside the loading dock at the Flushing rail yard with Rico and Luther Clay, looking over manifests as if they meant anything today. The real cargo wasn't on the train. It was in whispers and sideways glances. His crew was tense. Distracted. They felt it too—the ground shifting.

"He was Aldo's man," Rico said. "You think it was a message?"

Salvatore didn't answer immediately. He studied the men unloading crates, then the foreman fidgeting too much at the edge of the platform.

"I think it was leverage," he said.

"Yours or his?"

"That's what I intend to find out."

That afternoon, Salvatore sent two letters—one to Claudia Voss, requesting information on Victor's movements the week before; the other to a contact in the NYPD's vice squad, an officer on the take who occasionally "misplaced" autopsy reports for a fee.

The message was simple: *Find out who Victor met before he died. And who benefits from it.*

By sunset, the answer came back in pieces.

Victor had met with Nico DeMarco.

Twice.

Salvatore read the note three times.

"DeMarco's trying to split us," he said to Rosa that evening, spreading the notes across the dining table.

"Or set you up to think Aldo already has," she replied, tracing the pattern with her fingertip. "Either way, someone wants you to end the partnership for them."

"Why?"

Rosa folded her arms. "Because if you walk, you look volatile. If you stay, you look weak."

He nodded slowly.

"So we do neither."

The next day, Salvatore paid a visit to Father Leone.

He didn't come for confession. He came for clarity.

They sat in the pews of St. Anthony's, late morning light streaming through stained glass. No one else was in the church. Just the faint echo of the city outside.

"The people you're working with," the priest said, "they live by silence. By secrets. But that silence isn't peace."

"No," Salvatore said. "It's control."

Father Leone looked at him.

"And what are you controlling, Salvatore?"

He didn't answer right away.

Then, quietly: "How much blood it costs to keep what I've built."

The priest nodded, but didn't smile.

"Then count carefully."

Salvatore summoned Aldo two days later at the Cold House.

No messengers. No middlemen. Just one note, handwritten:

"You owe me one truth. I expect it in person." – S.V.

Aldo arrived late. Alone. Again.

The door slammed behind him.

"I thought we had terms," he said.

"We do," Salvatore replied. "But you forgot to include honesty."

Aldo's eyes darkened. "You accusing me of something?"

"I'm asking you if Victor met with DeMarco before he died."

Aldo blinked. Just once. But it was enough.

"I didn't authorize it," he said.

"Then you're losing control."

"I'm not."

Salvatore stepped forward, voice low.

"If I find out you let him play both sides, I'll cut the route in half. I'll take the Havana ports, and I'll leave you with rum and regrets."

Aldo's voice dropped to a growl. "You wouldn't last a week without me."

Salvatore leaned in. "You're not the only devil in this city, Aldo. You're just the one who doesn't know when the floor's about to collapse."

They stared at each other in silence.

Finally, Aldo reached into his coat and pulled out a folded envelope.

"Victor was trying to sell route intel. I was going to kill him myself. Someone beat me to it."

Salvatore took the envelope. Opened it.

Inside: maps, manifests, and a ledger of payoff drops to two DeMarco lieutenants.

Proof.

Insurance.

Or both.

"I came to you first," Aldo said. "Remember that."

Salvatore pocketed the file.

"Then act like it."

That night, Salvatore met with Luther, Rico, and Claudia in the basement beneath Eden.

He laid the folder on the table. Let them read.

When they finished, he said only one thing:

"We don't pull out. We don't back down. We move faster. Smarter. And if Aldo falters again, we bury him in the same hole they dug for Victor."

Salvatore stood at the window in the Sullivan Street flat as rain returned to Brooklyn.

Rosa joined him, brushing a strand of hair behind her ear.

"Well?" she asked.

"He gave me the truth. Or part of it."

"And if it's the wrong part?"

Salvatore didn't blink.

"Then I make sure I write the ending."

7

The Cop with No Badge

Part I - July, 1925 - Precinct 113, Rear Stairwell

The walls of the precinct sweated in the summer heat. Paint peeled like old scabs. Fluorescent bulbs hummed with a nervous buzz overhead. At this hour, the front desk was quiet. Civilians had gone home, drunks were still asleep in the alleyways, and the night shift hadn't yet soured their coffee.

Salvatore didn't come through the front.

He never did.

He slipped in through the rear stairwell—past the boiler room and the motor pool—and took the stairs two at a time until he reached the third floor, where a single metal door bore no name, just a scuffed window that hadn't seen a rag in years.

Inside, Officer Patrick O'Hara waited, coat off, sleeves rolled, whiskey already poured into a precinct mug.

"You're late," O'Hara said, not looking up from his desk.

"I was early," Salvatore replied. "I just didn't want to watch you drink alone."

The Irishman grunted, gestured at the chair across from him. "Sit. Talk."

Salvatore did.

O'Hara had been on the force for fifteen years. Long enough to stop pretending. He was the kind of cop who hadn't filed a clean report since the Wilson administration. His tie was always crooked, his shoes never polished, and his pension padded by names that never made it into arrest logs.

But he wasn't sloppy.

That's what made him valuable—and dangerous.

"You asked for a meeting," Salvatore said. "I assume that means something changed."

O'Hara leaned back, fingers laced behind his head.

"You're making too much noise."

"I'm making money. That's not the same."

"It is when it's loud enough for captains to start asking questions."

Salvatore crossed one leg over the other. "Then this is the part where I make them stop asking."

He slid a leather envelope across the table. Inside—$1,000 in mixed bills, crisp, folded, and untraceable.

O'Hara didn't touch it. Not yet.

Instead, he raised an eyebrow. "This buys what?"

"Silence. Time. And muscle. I don't want raids. I don't want my trucks pulled over unless they're running empty. And if someone starts sniffing around Harlem or Red Hook, I want to know before they ask questions."

O'Hara finally reached for the envelope, flipped through the bills without counting.

"This buys thirty days," he said flatly. "No more. I won't be the only blue shirt getting nervous."

Salvatore nodded. "Then we renegotiate in thirty."

"And if you miss a payment?"

"I won't."

O'Hara chuckled. "You're a confident bastard."

"No," Salvatore said. "I'm a punctual one."

They sat in silence for a few seconds. Then Salvatore added, almost casually:

"And in exchange, you'll keep your friends out of Aldo Rossi's pocket."

That got a reaction.

O'Hara's fingers stopped moving. The smirk faded.

"You think I work for Aldo?"

"I think Aldo thinks you do."

O'Hara tapped the mug against his desk. "You're a paranoid bastard, too."

"I'm a man who likes to know how many knives are in the room."

The officer leaned forward now, his tone more clipped. "You think I'm going to sell you out?"

"I think you already have. Once. I just haven't figured out when."

The two men stared at each other, silence pressing like a stone between them.

Then O'Hara reached into his drawer and pulled out a sealed folder. Tossed it onto the table.

"Names. Patrol routes. Officers who'll turn their heads. Judges who owe favors. You think I'm playing both sides? Read that and tell me who I'm betting on."

Salvatore opened the folder.

Inside: four pages of typed lists. Real. Dangerous. Useful.

"You made this for me?"

"I made it for the man who can keep paying," O'Hara said. "Right now, that's you."

Back in the car, Rico drove them through the misty side streets of Red Hook.

"You trust him?" Rico asked.

"No."

"Then why pay him?"

"Because he doesn't trust me either."

Rico nodded slowly. "Mutual blackmail. My favorite kind of alliance."

Salvatore looked out the window.

"It's not blackmail yet," he said. "But it's close."

Later that night, Salvatore met Rosa on the roof of the Sullivan Street flat. The city was quiet below, the smell of brick and salt thick in the air.

"You met with O'Hara," she said, not asking.

"I did."

"And?"

"He gave me what I needed."

She studied him. "And what did he take?"

Salvatore looked down at the street.

"He took my ability to pretend we're clean."

Rosa stepped beside him.

"We were never clean."

He turned to her, half-smiling. "Then at least now we're honest."

Part II - Three Days Later - Red Hook

Salvatore stood behind the counter of a closed butcher shop on Van Brunt Street, flipping through O'Hara's list.

He had memorized half of it already—names, beats, shifts. Officers willing to look the other way. A few judges with gambling debts. Even a customs inspector listed only as "Fisher – always needs rent."

It was useful.

Too useful.

Rico leaned on the meat scale beside him. "What do you want to hit first?"

"Not hit," Salvatore said. "Test."

He tapped a line on the second page.

"Officer Lang. Beats on Pacific Avenue. We push a shipment through his block tomorrow. Late. Two trucks. Marked wrong on the paperwork."

"You think he'll flag it?"

"I think if he does, we'll know this list isn't just fake—it's bait."

The next night, the trucks rolled at 2:13 a.m., headlights dimmed, rumbling through cobblestone alleys toward a locked warehouse near the pier. Each carried false manifests claiming they were delivering plumbing fixtures. Inside: 300 cases of Canadian rye.

Officer Lang watched from his patrol car.

He didn't move.

Didn't call it in.

Didn't flinch.

By 2:25 a.m., the trucks were parked, unloaded, and the

liquor hidden beneath crates of actual plumbing equipment Salvatore had bought just for the ruse.

Rico reported it with a grin. "Lang didn't blink."

Salvatore nodded. "One down."

Over the next five days, they tested seven more names on O'Hara's list.

Each one passed.

One even tipped off Salvatore in advance—Officer Grady, walking his beat near Clinton Street, slipped a note under the bakery door:

"*Vice is moving uptown. Three cars. Avoid 7th Ave. – G.*"

Grady had never met Salvatore in person.

And now he wouldn't have to.

He'd just bought himself two more months of safety.

But not everything added up.

O'Hara's list had value, no doubt. But it also had… gaps.

A name would be missing from a beat. A precinct would suddenly reassign a loyal officer to desk duty with no explanation. A judge marked as compromised handed down a harsher-than-expected sentence in a narcotics case.

Salvatore circled each anomaly in red ink. Ten of them, by week's end.

"Something's wrong," he told Rosa as she cooked dinner, slicing onions with precise rhythm.

She didn't look up. "You're getting what you paid for."

"No," he said. "I'm getting what *he* wanted me to see."

She glanced over. "You think the list was curated?"

"Worse," Salvatore replied. "I think it's alive."

Rosa set down the knife. "Explain."

"He's updating it. Feeding it based on our moves. Watching who we use. Who we avoid. Who we test. He's not just selling protection."

"He's selling us."

That night, Salvatore met with Claudia Voss at Eden.

The speakeasy hummed with low music and high whispers. Beneath the din, in a private booth, Salvatore laid out the pattern.

"He gave us intel that works," he said, "but not all of it. And not for free. Every officer we touch is a breadcrumb."

"Which means someone's following the trail," Claudia said.

Salvatore nodded. "And when they get to the end, we're standing there with our pockets full."

"Could be the Feds. Could be Internal Affairs. Could even be Lombardi's people watching through a badge."

Claudia tapped her nails against her glass.

"You need a cleaner line."

"I need a mirror."

She raised an eyebrow. "You want me to turn the tables?"

"I want to know what O'Hara does when he thinks no one's watching."

Claudia smiled. "I know just the girl."

Her name was Tess Malone.

Twenty-three. Jazz singer by night. Informant by necessity. Her brother had a two-year sentence hanging over his head for stabbing a numbers runner with a fork. Tess had made a deal with Claudia months ago to avoid losing him to Sing Sing.

Now, she was back in play.

Two nights later, she walked into O'Hara's favorite back-room poker club in Flatbush, wearing red silk and desperation. She played dumb. Flirted easy. Laughed too much.

By the end of the night, she was sitting on the armrest of O'Hara's chair, sipping rye from his glass.

Three hours later, she had the name of a second buyer.

Inspector Calvin Dorsey – Manhattan Vice Division.

She passed it to Claudia. Claudia passed it to Salvatore.

Rico read it aloud and frowned.

"Dorsey? He's on the take?"

"He's on *O'Hara's* take," Salvatore said.

Rico blinked. "O'Hara's not just the middleman. He's building something."

"Or someone else is building it through him."

Salvatore folded the name into his notebook.

"We just became a test case."

Back at Sullivan Street, Rosa stitched the names together on a string map.

O'Hara. Grady. Lang. Dorsey. Gaps filled in. Red lines crossed over blue ones. Patterns emerged.

"You see it?" she asked.

Salvatore did.

O'Hara's not just feeding them a list—he's watching who bites. Tracking reactions. Building a second ledger somewhere. A bigger one.

"Why not burn us?" Rosa asked. "Why keep the game alive?"

"Because we're the strongest piece on the board," Salvatore replied. "No one wants the king off the table... until they know who takes the crown."

Part III - Just Before Midnight - East River Pier

Officer Patrick O'Hara hated meetings near the river. It smelled like iron and old regrets. But when Salvatore Vitali asked for a quiet place with no ears, he wasn't just being cautious. He was declaring intent.

And when a man like Salvatore declares anything, you show up.

O'Hara lit a cigarette under a hanging bulb as the river lapped against rusted pylons. He wore no badge tonight—just a brown trench coat, his pistol visible but unthreatening.

Salvatore emerged from the shadows alone.

"I thought you always traveled with your watchdog," O'Hara said.

"Not when I'm asking questions I don't want him to hear the answers to."

O'Hara took a drag. "Then ask."

Salvatore stepped into the light. His expression was calm, but his voice was a razor.

"How long have you been feeding names to Dorsey?"

O'Hara didn't flinch. "Who says I have?"

"I do."

A beat passed.

O'Hara blew smoke sideways. "Longer than you've been moving liquor. He pays regular. Doesn't whine. Keeps quiet."

"You sold him my crew."

"I gave him shadows. Not bodies."

"Don't split hairs with me."

O'Hara's jaw flexed. "You think you're clean, Vitali? You think paying me makes you untouchable? You're one name in a city full of them. I protect you, sure. But I also protect *me*."

Salvatore didn't look away.

"And when Dorsey decides I'm no longer useful?"

O'Hara shrugged. "Then I stop protecting you."

"Then you start dying," Salvatore said flatly.

O'Hara's eyes narrowed.

"You threatening a cop?"

"No," Salvatore replied. "I'm promising a reckoning."

He pulled a folded piece of paper from his pocket and held it out.

O'Hara hesitated.

"Take it," Salvatore said.

The officer snatched it, opened it.

Inside: a photo—grainy, taken through a club window. O'Hara seated beside a well-known bookmaker with three unsolved murders tied to his name.

"You think I'm the only one who plays dirty?" Salvatore said. "I'm not. But I'm the only one who cleans up after."

O'Hara lowered the paper slowly.

"You made a copy?"

"I made five."

"Where are they?"

"With people who hate surprises."

The silence dragged.

Then O'Hara chuckled. It wasn't warm.

"You always were dangerous."

Salvatore stepped closer. "You don't know what I am."

O'Hara pointed the cigarette toward him.

"Then tell me."

Salvatore didn't blink.

"I'm the man you can't afford to lose and can't afford to

cross. You want to keep your pension, your quiet house, your liver intact? Then you follow my rules. Not Dorsey's. Not the city's. *Mine.*"

O'Hara didn't respond. But he didn't deny it either.

He just nodded.

"Understood."

A few days later at the flat, Rico entered holding a new folder, eyebrows raised.

"You got him."

Salvatore took the folder. Inside—new patrol rotations, deeper bribe connections, even two addresses linked to Dorsey's side business in Manhattan.

"You pushed him too hard," Rico said. "You sure he won't fold?"

"He's not a soldier," Salvatore replied. "He's a survivor. And survivors are easiest to trap. They're too scared to run and too smart to get shot."

Rico grinned. "You always think ten steps ahead?"

"No," Salvatore said. "But I know who will walk into mine."

8

Blood in the Alley

Part I - August, 1925 – Lower Manhattan, East 4th and Bowery

The deal was supposed to be routine.

Two crates of bonded Irish whiskey, exchanged for a stack of bearer bonds with cleaned serials—half the price, twice the profit. Neutral ground. Fast hands. Familiar faces.

But nothing about that night went as planned.

The first sign was the air, too quiet for Lower Manhattan. No cats in the alley. No passing cars. Even the usual drunk from the corner stoop had vanished. The second sign was how long they waited. Rico started getting more nervous as the seconds ticked by.

Luca Vitale glanced at his watch again. 11:42.

"Where the hell are they?" he muttered.

Beside him, Gio Ferrara shook a cigarette from a metal case. "Lombardis don't wait. Which means they're already watching."

Gio had been right.

The bullets came before the first handshake.

Two from the alley. One from a second-story window. Luca dropped instantly, blood blooming from his chest. Gio returned fire, clipped a shadow, but the car peeled away before backup arrived.

By the time the scene quieted, Luca was gone.

Salvatore stood in silence while Rico detailed the shooting a few hours later at the Sullivan Street flat. The blood on his coat had already dried. The pistol on the table hadn't been fired—it had only been held. Rico's hands trembled as he spoke.

"They were waiting. It was a setup. No other explanation."

Salvatore didn't speak. He didn't blink.

He walked to the window, stared out at a city lit in guilt and gasoline.

"I want names," he said.

Rico nodded. "I've already got two. Nicky Prano and a runner named Sal Lombardi. Both low-tier, but they were seen in the area."

Salvatore turned.

"I don't want runners."

"I know."

"Then get me *blood*."

The call went out at dawn.

Within six hours, two men were pulled off a poker table in Bensonhurst and dragged into an alley. One was released after a warning. The other lost two fingers and a tongue.

The message was sent.

But Salvatore wasn't done.

Claudia Voss arranged the meeting that night in Midtown, underneath the Edison Hotel—discreet, quiet, tucked into the back office of a failing cabaret. Inside, Salvatore met with Samuele Lombardi, cousin to Marco, mid-tier enforcer, and the kind of man who only survived this long by knowing when to speak and when to beg.

Salvatore didn't give him time for either.

"You set us up."

"I didn't—"

"You knew they were coming."

"I swear on my mother's grave—"

"Your mother's in a nursing home in Jersey."

Samuele froze.

Salvatore stepped closer.

"You sold out a deal and cost me a man. That's not a debt. That's a *funeral*."

He nodded to Rico.

Rico didn't hesitate.

A single shot. Behind the ear. No theatrics.

Clean.

Public enough to be seen.

Quiet enough to be questioned.

The news reached the Lombardis before the blood dried.

Marco didn't call.

He didn't send a man.

He didn't have to.

He sent a body.

Dropped at the doorstep of Eden, wrapped in butcher paper,

chest carved with a single word:

"ENOUGH."

Rosa found Salvatore in the study that evening, unfolding the paper without expression.

"You started a war," she said.

"I answered one."

"They'll hit back harder."

"They always do."

She moved to the window, arms folded.

"What now?"

Salvatore leaned on the desk.

"We give them what they want."

Rosa turned, startled. "What they want?"

"A reason to stop."

She frowned. "And what's that?"

Salvatore lit a match. Burned the butcher paper over a metal ashtray.

"Fear."

Tourists strolled, vendors hawked saltwater taffy, and jazz poured from the radios of beachside cafés a few days later on the Coney Island Boardwalk.

At precisely 12:07 p.m., a man named Dominic "Little Dom" Serretti, Lombardi loan shark and longtime mid-level collector, was shot four times while exiting a shoeshine stand near the Wonder Wheel.

Witnesses screamed.

Children ran.

Blood painted the wooden slats of the boardwalk.

The shooter—unmasked—walked calmly away, blending

into the panicked crowd before slipping down a side street and disappearing into a stolen cab.

The press called it madness.

The underworld called it a statement.

The Vitalis called it closure.

Back at the Sullivan Street flat, Salvatore stood over the ledger, updating names.

Two crossed out.

Three circled.

He didn't flinch.

But his hands moved slower now.

"You good?" Rico asked.

Salvatore nodded. "We're even."

"For now."

"For now."

Part II - Two Days Later - Green-Wood Cemetery, Brooklyn

Rain clung to the stones like sweat.

A small crowd gathered under slate skies as Luca Vitale's coffin was lowered into the earth. No priest spoke. No hymns played. It wasn't that kind of funeral. In their world, grief was private. Vengeance was public.

Salvatore stood still, collar turned up, watching the casket descend like it might rise again if stared at long enough.

Rico stood beside him, face raw with silent fury. Gio Ferrara smoked a cigarette without looking at anything in particular.

A few others from the crew loitered near the gates, posted, alert, because no one was sure this wasn't another trap.

Rosa had offered to come. Salvatore told her no.

Luca had been Rico's closest friend. That grief didn't belong to family. It belonged to men who'd bled in the same cars, run the same alleys, buried the same mistakes.

When the dirt hit the coffin, Rico flinched like it had hit his own ribs.

"He was twenty-nine," he muttered.

Salvatore said nothing.

Rico's jaw tightened. "We should've hit harder."

"We hit enough."

"Not for him."

Salvatore turned. "You want to burn the city for one man?"

"I want them to feel what I felt when I saw his face."

Salvatore studied him. "Then survive long enough to look them in the eye when they do."

The meeting was called in whispers at the Cold House.

Salvatore, Rico, Gio, Luther Clay, and Claudia Voss sat around a battered steel table in the freezer room where a single bulb buzzed above.

"We're being baited," Claudia said. "Lombardi's trying to drag you into a war."

"He already did," Rico snapped.

"But not on the books," she replied. "A sit-down hasn't been called. No formal vote. No territory challenged. They're hoping you make the next move bloody."

Salvatore nodded. "Because then they get to play victim."

"And paint you as a rogue," Luther added. "Which gives Mancini or Russo the excuse to isolate you."

"Divide and conquer," Claudia murmured.

Rico leaned forward, arms on the table.

"So what? We sit on our hands?"

"No," Salvatore said. "We prepare. Quietly."

He tossed a folded map onto the table.

"Their next shipment comes in Friday. Cigarettes from Georgia through a warehouse in Jersey City."

"You want to hit it?" Gio asked.

"No. I want to *buy* it."

Claudia blinked. "From who?"

"From the *drivers*," Salvatore said. "They're underpaid and overworked. We offer double cash, no questions. We intercept the load, send it back—untouched."

Rico frowned. "We give it back?"

Salvatore smiled faintly.

"And include a note: *Wrong address. Try again.*"

Two days later, three Lombardi trucks sat idling near a loading dock in Jersey City; their drivers smoking and complaining about pay cuts and overnight shifts. Two men approached in mechanic jumpsuits, flashed bundles of cash, and spoke in low, friendly tones.

No threats. No guns.

Fifteen minutes later, the trucks pulled away—still carrying their load—but rerouted.

The next morning, they arrived back at the Lombardi warehouse with a hand-written envelope taped to the dashboard.

Inside:

"No need for bullets. Just better directions. – S.V."

The underworld response was instant.

Whispers spread.
Not about blood.
About brains.
Salvatore Vitali hadn't lost his edge—he'd sharpened it.

Salvatore sat at the desk in his study that night, ledger open, pouring over lists of names, numbers, and distribution routes. Rosa brought him coffee but didn't interrupt.

"Everyone thinks you're building to something," she said finally.

"I am."

"But not what they think."

He looked up.

"I'm not building a war," he said. "I'm building inevitability."

She nodded.

"And what happens when they finally corner you? When they call you to that table and demand blood or surrender?"

Salvatore stirred the coffee once, then let the spoon rest.

"Then I remind them I've already seen what's on the other side of surrender."

Meanwhile, at the Lombardi Estate in Staten Island, Marco Lombardi read the note three times.

His consigliere stood nearby, silent, waiting for a command that didn't come.

"He's smarter than I gave him credit for," Marco finally said.

"He made you look soft."

Marco nodded slowly.

"Then maybe it's time we remind everyone what my family's really made of."

Part III - Four Days Later - Staten Island, Lombardi Estate

The retaliation didn't come through muscle.

It came through silence.

Then pressure.

Then a name.

Salvatore received the news from Claudia Voss during an early morning call. Her voice was tight, measured.

"They flipped one of your men," she said. "I don't know who yet, but it's real. Something changed. Marco's people are walking with a different rhythm. You can feel it."

Salvatore didn't ask how she knew. She had her ways—dancers, waiters, barmaids with sharper eyes than half the police force.

He hung up without a word.

Then he called Rico.

Rain spit against the windows that afternoon as the crew assembled in the kitchen of Salvatore's flat.

Rico. Gio. Luther Clay. Frankie Romano. Even Massimo, pulled from his usual route in Queens.

Salvatore stood at the head of the table, arms folded.

"One of ours is talking," he said.

No one blinked.

No one denied.

Rico tensed. "You got a name?"

"No," Salvatore said. "But I've narrowed it."

He held up three files. Each with a name, address, movement logs, and last week's assignment notes.

Frankie frowned. "You think it's one of us?"

"No," Salvatore said. "But I think it's someone *just outside* the circle. Someone close enough to hear—but not close enough to bleed for it."

"Crew boss? Driver?" Luther asked.

"Maybe," Salvatore replied. "Maybe not."

Rico took a file, scanned it. "Tony Gallo?"

Salvatore nodded. "Disappeared for twelve hours last Tuesday. Claimed mechanical issues. No one verified."

Gio took another. "Maurice Dell?"

"Made two unannounced stops in Manhattan. One of them was six blocks from a known Lombardi book front."

Massimo slapped the table. "Then let's drag them both in and squeeze the truth out."

Salvatore shook his head.

"No fear. No noise. Not yet."

He looked around the table.

"We do this smart. Quiet. If Marco wants to rot us from the inside, then we smoke out the decay, piece by piece."

Tony Gallo arrived for what he thought was a routine pickup at the Cold House that night.

Instead, he found Massimo and Gio waiting.

They didn't beat him.

They didn't shout.

They asked questions—soft, repetitive, invasive.

Where were you Tuesday?

Who did you meet in Hell's Kitchen?

Why did you skip check-in in Flatbush?

Tony had answers.

Too many.

Each word layered with details.

Too neat.

Too rehearsed.

Massimo leaned in, voice like gravel. "You're sweating, Tony. And it ain't the ice."

Tony broke at the fourth question.

It wasn't him.

But he knew who it was.

Maurice Dell.

"He's got a cousin married to Marco's sister," Tony whispered. "They meet every other week. Says it's family. Says he's clean. But I seen him with that Lombardi punk, Nicky Prano. Swear it."

Salvatore didn't wait.

Maurice was pulled that night outside a bar in Bensonhurst.

He was given a choice.

A car ride and an explanation.

Or a ditch and none.

He took the ride.

Rico drove.

Salvatore sat beside him.

Maurice stammered. Denied. Cried.

Then confessed.

"They offered me money. Said it wasn't real betrayal. Just updates. Just movement. Just *logistics*—that's what they said. Just a few details. Nothing about you. Nothing personal."

Salvatore stared at him.

"You gave them our drop schedule."

Maurice's lip trembled. "I didn't know—"

"You *knew*."

"I needed the money."

Salvatore nodded.

"That's always the first excuse."

Maurice Dell's body was found behind an abandoned church in Gravesend, shot twice through the chest. No signature. No note.

Just silence.

And the return of fear.

The next morning, Claudia called again.

"They're quiet," she said. "Lombardi's crew is stepping carefully."

"Because they know what I know," Salvatore said. "And what I'll do with it."

She paused.

"And what *will* you do?"

Salvatore didn't answer immediately.

Then:

"I'll make them call the meeting."

"You won't request it?"

"No," he said. "They'll beg for it."

Salvatore sat at the table in the flat alone, the files spread before him, red ink marking routes, shifts, and damage done.

Rosa walked in, barefoot, quiet.

"You lost someone else?" she asked.

"Yes."

"And you don't look angry."

"I'm not."

"Why?"

"Because now," Salvatore said, "they know I'm not chasing

blood. I'm controlling it."

She touched his shoulder.

"And the next move?"

He looked up.

"They'll call a sit-down. And when they do, they'll think they're calling a truce."

She raised an eyebrow. "And what are they really calling?"

Salvatore smiled—cold, thin, unyielding.

"A coronation."

9

The Price of Power

Part I - Late August, 1925 - Manhattan, The Waldorf Room

The room smelled like old money and older sins.

Wood-paneled walls, a chandelier the size of a piano, cigar smoke that didn't rise so much as settle. The Waldorf Room hadn't seen a wedding or banquet in years. Now, it served only one purpose: negotiation among men who didn't ask permission to run New York.

The table was circular. Always circular. No one sat at the head, but since DeMarco's disappearance, everyone knew where power rested—usually wherever Carlo Mancini's chair happened to be.

Tonight, though, everyone kept glancing at Salvatore Vitali.

He wore a gray suit, pressed and quiet, no pinstripes, no jewelry, no rings—only the iron signet Rosa had given him, gleaming against his finger like a silent oath.

Carlo spoke first.

"Thank you for coming, gentlemen."

They all knew why they were there.

Antonio Russo, older now, breathing hard through a silk handkerchief, muttered something about "preserving stability." Marco Lombardi didn't speak. He just stared, arms folded, the faintest grin tugging at the corner of his mouth.

Vincent DeMarco was absent again. His chair sat empty, like a ghost presiding over the gathering.

Salvatore noted that carefully.

Carlo cleared his throat.

"We've had enough blood to drown a bishop these past few months. The press is getting noisy. The Feds are getting curious. And some of our... mutual arrangements are getting fragile."

No one disagreed.

"Which is why," Carlo continued, "we're putting forward a vote. A fifth seat. The Vitali family, led by Salvatore Vitali, will be granted full status—equal vote, equal cut."

Salvatore didn't blink. He knew it was coming.

But the pause told him there was more.

Carlo looked to Marco.

Marco looked to Salvatore.

"There's one condition," Marco said. "A gesture. To prove you're not just sharp, but loyal."

Salvatore kept his hands folded.

"I don't work on consignment."

Marco smiled thinly. "It's not work. It's *alignment.*"

Carlo sighed. "There's a man. A problem. Inside the DeMarco family. One of their capos. Young. Too ambitious. Too vocal. He's trying to rally the old loyalists and sweep in once Vincent dies."

Salvatore already knew the name before they said it.

Gianni Palma.

Carlo said it anyway.

"You'll take the seat. You'll take the power. But only if you remove Palma quietly. Publicly. Permanently."

Salvatore leaned back in his chair.

"You want me to kill him now?"

Carlo shook his head. "We're not savages."

Marco snorted.

"Soon," Carlo said. "Clean. Loud enough to be heard. Quiet enough to vanish in the morning papers."

"And if I refuse?"

Carlo's voice lowered.

"Then you remain what you are. A respected outsider. Useful. Feared. But never equal."

A long silence followed.

Then Salvatore stood.

He didn't speak.

He didn't agree.

He just left.

Rico drove, eyes flicking to the rearview mirror every other block.

"You're quiet."

"I'm thinking."

"They really want you to kill Palma?"

Salvatore nodded.

"Why him?"

"He's too smart for them. Too independent. He's trying to revive DeMarco's strength—and if he succeeds, he'll challenge the whole balance."

"So they want you to cut his throat and take the chair."

Salvatore looked out the window.

"No. They want me to *prove* I'll bleed for the table before I sit at it."

Rico's knuckles tightened on the wheel.

"You gonna do it?"

"I'm going to *decide*."

Rosa was already pouring wine when Salvatore returned. She placed the glass in front of him and waited.

"Well?"

"They offered it."

She didn't smile. She knew better.

"And?"

"They want Palma gone."

Rosa sat.

"That's not a request."

"No," he said. "It's a blueprint."

She took a slow sip, watching him over the rim.

"You could refuse."

"I could."

"You'd live."

"But never *rule*."

A long pause.

Then she said: "So you're going to kill him."

Salvatore didn't answer.

Instead, he said: "I'm going to look him in the eye first."

The next day, Salvatore arrived in Harlem at Palma's speakeasy. The club was loud, all brass and velvet, packed with dancers and smoke. Salvatore didn't bring Rico. He didn't need him.

This wasn't a hit. This was reconnaissance.

Palma was in a back booth, surrounded by two men and a woman with red lipstick and the stance of someone carrying a gun under her coat.

He smiled when Salvatore approached.

"You came."

Salvatore sat across from him. No handshake.

"You know why."

Palma nodded.

"They want me dead."

"Yes."

"And you want the seat."

"I want stability."

Palma laughed. "Same thing."

Then he leaned forward.

"They think I'll fight them. I won't. Not yet. But I will *outlive* them. And that's what scares them."

Salvatore said nothing.

"You could kill me," Palma said. "Or you could let me live. Let me climb. Let me owe you."

Salvatore stared at him.

Palma shrugged.

"But if you *don't* kill me, they'll come for you next. Because once they see you hesitate, you stop being scary."

Salvatore stood.

"I didn't come to ask your permission."

Palma tilted his head. "Then what?"

Salvatore's eyes narrowed.

"To see if you deserved to live."

Part II - Following Night - Sullivan Street Flat

The lamp buzzed low on the desk, casting gold across the page. Salvatore stared at a list of names—capos, lieutenants, earners. Palma's name was circled. Twice.

Rosa sat across from him, barefoot, legs tucked under her in quiet defiance of the violence they were discussing.

"You believe him?" she asked.

"I believe he thinks he can outplay them," Salvatore replied.

"And can he?"

"Maybe."

"Then why not let him?"

"Because the seat's real," Salvatore said. "And it's open. And if I don't take it, someone else will. Someone with less patience and more bodies."

She tilted her head. "You want the power?"

"I want the leverage."

Rosa leaned forward. "So take it. But don't do it the way they want."

Salvatore blinked. "You think I should let him live?"

"No," she said. "I think you should decide what his death *means*."

Two days later, Salvatore met with Luther Clay and Claudia Voss in a private booth behind Eden, the hum of jazz from the next room bleeding through velvet curtains.

"I need a message," Salvatore said. "One that makes it clear I've taken the seat—but not on their terms."

Luther nodded slowly. "You want it loud enough to echo, but clean enough to be called politics."

"Exactly."

Claudia crossed her legs. "Palma's got enemies. You make it look like one of *them* pulled the trigger—Lombardi, Mancini, even internal DeMarco rats—you turn his death into another family's liability."

Salvatore smiled faintly. "Can you plant that?"

Claudia returned the smile. "By the end of the week, the city will believe Palma was about to flip… until someone made sure he couldn't."

Rico adjusted the scope on the Remington rifle on the rooftop as Salvatore watched from the shadows outside Palma's club.

"You sure you don't want it messy?" Rico asked.

"No," Salvatore said. "This isn't about rage."

"What is it about?"

Salvatore answered softly.

"Inheritance."

Palma stepped onto the balcony below, alone, cigarette glowing in the dark.

Rico lined up the shot.

Paused.

"Still want me to pull it?"

Salvatore nodded once.

Rico exhaled.

The shot cracked like a branch snapping in a quiet forest.

Palma's body dropped in silence.

Salvatore returned to the Waldorf Room a few days later, alone.

Carlo Mancini was waiting, eyes tired but shrewd. Marco Lombardi stood at the bar, pouring a drink he didn't offer to anyone else. Antonio Russo dozed quietly in his seat, hand twitching from an old war wound.

Carlo looked up. "It's done?"

Salvatore sat.

"It's done."

No cheers. No smiles.

Just acknowledgment.

Marco raised his glass. "Welcome to the table."

Antonio grunted. "'Bout time."

Carlo opened a ledger and passed it across the table. Salvatore flipped it open—distribution rights, territory lines, arbitration clauses, voting rules.

The seat was real.

So was the responsibility.

Carlo offered a pen.

Salvatore signed.

No flourish. Just ink on a line.

A contract sealed in blood, but bound by strategy.

Salvatore poured two glasses of whiskey and handed one to Rosa that night when he got home.

"It's done," he said.

She raised her glass. "To the seat?"

He shook his head.

"To the distance between us and the next man who thinks he can take it."

Marco Lombardi read the morning paper three times at his estate in Staten Island.

"DeMarco Capo Slain in Suspected Internal Dispute."

No mention of Vitali.

No ties to the Families.

No footprints.

He poured himself another drink and smiled.

"Maybe he's not just dangerous," Marco muttered. "Maybe he's *smart.*"

His consigliere leaned forward. "Should we be worried?"

Marco smirked.

"Not yet."

But his hand tightened on the glass.

Claudia stood near the bar of the Eden, scanning the room.

A pair of DeMarco soldiers were already whispering about loyalty. A Mancini bookman had just requested a meeting. The Russo crew's best enforcer was asking if Claudia knew someone who could move crates quieter than Lombardi's men.

The power had shifted.

No bullets required.

Just a single death.

And a very public silence.

Part III - One Week Later - Midtown, Private Dining Room at La Campanella

The table was smaller this time. Tighter. Five chairs, five names, one empty seat still for Vincent DeMarco.

Salvatore sat to Carlo Mancini's right now, not by tradition, but by design. It was a signal. A crown not worn, but recognized.

A waiter cleared the first course while no one spoke.

Finally, Antonio Russo broke the silence.

"You made your point, Vitali," he said. "Clean. Quiet. Palma's death didn't even make it to the second page."

Salvatore said nothing. He didn't need to. His seat spoke for him now.

Marco Lombardi leaned forward, swirling wine in his glass. "So. Now that we're all… aligned. Let's talk expansion."

Carlo nodded. "Florida."

Antonio raised an eyebrow. "Cuban ports?"

"Already soft. Too many hands. But inland? The railroads. Distribution hubs. Tampa's dirty enough to be useful."

Marco shrugged. "And we need a footprint down south."

Carlo turned to Salvatore.

"You know the docks better than any of us. You get the first look. If it's viable, you lay the foundation."

It wasn't a favor. It was a test.

Salvatore nodded. "I'll send Clay and Navarro. Quiet eyes first. Then cargo."

Marco smiled thinly. "You send the right message."

Salvatore met his gaze.

"I send results."

The night air was thick with humidity and something heavier—expectation. Salvatore met Rico after the meeting outside of La Campanella.

Rico leaned against the car, chewing a toothpick, watching the door.

"Well?" he asked as Salvatore approached.

"They want me to build south."

"Why you?"

"Because if I fail, they lose nothing. If I succeed, they gain everything."

Rico spit the toothpick.

"And you?"

"I get to see who tries to take it from me once I do."

Rosa finished lighting the candles on the dinner table. Two glasses of red, fresh bread, the scent of garlic rising from the kitchen. It almost felt like home.

But Salvatore's shoulders were tighter. His tie was still on. His eyes were still far away.

"They giving you the runaround?" she asked.

"No," he said. "They're giving me opportunity."

"But not trust."

He looked at her.

"Power doesn't trust. It trades. One hand to hold. One knife to keep behind the back."

Rosa sat. "And what's your knife?"

Salvatore raised his glass.

"You."

Antonio Russo wheezed between sentences, but his words still carried in the halls of the Russo estate..

"Keep an eye on him," he told his consigliere. "The boy's smart, but too fast. He cuts corners that the rest of us paved."

The consigliere nodded. "You want him slowed down?"

"No," Russo said. "I want him *predictable*."

Marco stared at a city map tacked to the wall in his estate— routes, pins, names in red.

He lit a fresh cigarette.

"Let him think he's king," he said to no one in particular.

"Let him build his castle."
He exhaled smoke like a sigh.
"Then we'll see who burns it first."

II

Act II

Smoke and Steel

10

The Baptism of Violence

Part I - September 1925 - Brooklyn, Late Afternoon

The sound of industry filled the harbor—cranes creaking, chains snapping taut, the dull bark of foremen yelling over the churn of the tide. A freight ship from Savannah offloaded cargo onto the docks below, marked with new codes, routed under new authority.

Salvatore Vitali stood at the edge of Pier 14, hands in his coat pockets, watching as the work unfolded. This was no longer Mancini or Russo territory—not officially. The logistics company painted on the crates was clean. The warehouse upstream had been leased under an alias Rosa had created through a series of paper companies.

This was Vitali land now.

And no one even knew it yet.

Rico Navarro appeared at his side, wiping sweat from his brow with the back of his sleeve.

"We just cleared the second hold. Clay's boys are pulling the paperwork through Jersey. No flags."

Salvatore nodded. "The rail line?"

"Still negotiating. But the foreman likes whiskey. We'll be friends by next Tuesday."

Salvatore didn't smile, but the corner of his mouth twitched—approval, in his own language.

"And the Florida situation?"

"Quiet," Rico said. "Which is the best kind. Claudia's got ears in Tampa already. They're willing to look the other way for a cut. Maybe ten percent, tops."

Salvatore stepped back from the edge and lit a cigarette. "They'll get seven."

"Sure you don't want to walk in like a friend?"

"No," Salvatore said. "I want them to think I *might* be."

The crew met in the freezer room, surrounded by crates of imported goods, some real, some not. Luther Clay laid out the new distribution routes across a chalkboard propped against a stack of Cuban rum. Gio Ferrara hovered over a clipboard, tracking delivery schedules in Queens. Massimo leaned back on a crate, chewing sunflower seeds with the calm of a man who'd already drawn three pistols today.

"This right here," Luther said, tapping the map near the waterfront, "gives us a back door through Port Elizabeth. It's low traffic. Less oversight."

"And whose toes does that step on?" Gio asked.

"Technically?" Luther shrugged. "Nobody. Legally? Every-one."

Salvatore approached the board and circled two zones in red.

"These warehouses—change the codes. They're too consistent. Anyone watching our paper will notice."

Rico added, "We should spread out the suppliers. Start moving crates through Irish and Jewish fronts. Less pattern, more noise."

"Do it," Salvatore said.

Claudia stepped in from the stairwell, trench coat still damp with rain.

"You've got ten days before Mancini's men try to probe the paperwork. One of their lieutenants reached out to a customs broker in Newark."

Salvatore turned. "Do we have a line on the broker?"

"I already bought his dog," she said dryly. "The man will follow."

There was laughter, short and quiet.

Salvatore nodded.

"Then we stay ahead. We move fast, but clean. No dust, no blood. We own this city when they're still trying to count crates."

The storm hit after midnight on Sullivan Street. Rain like nails, wind hissing between windowsills.

Salvatore stood in the kitchen, still in his shirt sleeves, reading the final ledger. Rosa approached in silence, a cup of coffee in one hand.

"You built a lot today," she said.

"Not enough."

"You never say 'enough.'"

He looked up. "I don't believe in it."

She slid the cup toward him. "Then what's this chapter for, Salvatore?"

He considered the question, fingers resting on the edge of

the ledger.

"It's the pause before the war," he said. "The moment you decide what kind of empire you're willing to protect—and what kind you'll burn to keep."

Rosa sat opposite him.

"Do you know which kind you're building?"

He didn't answer.

Not yet.

Antonio Russo coughed into a silk handkerchief, blood speckling the white cloth.

His consigliere poured him bourbon without asking.

"He's moving fast," Russo muttered. "Too fast."

"You gave him the south."

"I gave him a corridor," Russo said sharply. "Not a kingdom."

The consigliere waited.

"Call DeMarco," Russo said. "Find out who's still loyal."

"To DeMarco?"

Russo's eyes narrowed.

"To *anyone* not named Vitali."

Meanwhile, in the backroom of the Calico Room, Marco Lombardi drank alone, staring at a shipment manifest that bore the unmistakable signature of a Vitali broker. It was clean. Too clean.

His brother, Carmine, paced nearby.

"We said let him build," Carmine said.

Marco didn't look up.

"We didn't say how tall."

He leaned back, letting the silence hang like smoke.

"Keep watching," he said.

"And if he overreaches?"

Marco smiled coldly.

"Then we remind him who taught this city how to reach."

Part II - Two Days Later – Jersey City Rail Yards

The freight yard at dawn was a place of organized chaos—steel groaning under weight, engines hissing in clouds of vapor, men barking orders through clenched teeth and cigarettes. The movement looked random to outsiders, but to Salvatore, it was choreography.

This yard now moved on his timing.

Inside the foreman's shed, Rico stood beside two Tampa men—weather-beaten faces, southern drawls turned sharp by northern suspicion. They'd brought manifests, contract terms, and expectations.

Salvatore sat at a steel desk, flipping through the documents.

"You want fifteen percent," he said without looking up.

"Ten, if we run it through our trucks," the older one, Mason, replied.

Salvatore closed the folder. "You'll take six. We'll provide the drivers and route protection. You get paid on time, in full, and you don't lose any men to Miami politics."

The two men exchanged glances.

"And if we say no?"

Salvatore smiled, just barely.

"You won't."

They didn't.

The deal was sealed over a bottle of rye and a handshake

that meant more than ink. Salvatore never wrote what didn't need to be said.

Later that night in the backroom of the Eden, Gio Ferrara leaned over the route logs, a cigar burning beside his glass of gin. Claudia Voss stood by the window, counting delivery points aloud from memory. Luther Clay walked a slow circle around the table, drawing lines on a chalk map.

Everyone was moving.

Everyone but Frankie Romano.

He leaned against the back wall, arms crossed, eyes darting.

Salvatore noticed.

He always noticed.

After the others cleared out, he waved Rico off and nodded to Frankie.

"Sit."

Frankie did—slowly.

Salvatore lit a cigarette, took his time with the first drag.

"You've been quiet."

"Just listening."

"Always dangerous in a room full of people who expect noise."

Frankie shrugged. "Don't like Tampa."

"Not your first time complaining about it."

"It's not a complaint," Frankie said. "It's a concern."

Salvatore leaned back.

"Then share it."

Frankie hesitated. Not from fear—Salvatore would've respected that more. This was something else. Calculation. Maybe even guilt.

"We're moving too fast," Frankie said. "Too many trucks.

Too many ports. You're stretching the crew thin. We've got loyalty now, but if something goes wrong—if one deal folds, one driver flips—we're not tight enough to handle the fallout."

Salvatore exhaled slowly.

"You worried about the drivers?"

"I'm worried about *us*."

A long pause.

Then: "Who put that idea in your head?"

Frankie blinked. "No one."

"Then it was already there," Salvatore said.

Frankie frowned. "I'm loyal."

Salvatore nodded. "I know. That's why you're still sitting here."

"But?"

"But loyalty and doubt don't sleep well in the same bed."

Frankie stood, jaw clenched. "I said what I needed to."

"And I heard it," Salvatore replied calmly. "Now go get some rest."

Rosa found Salvatore pacing in the study later that night, cigarette burned to the filter.

"Frankie?"

"He's fidgeting."

"You think he's flipped?"

"No," Salvatore said. "I think he's scared."

Rosa sat at the desk, flipping through the ledger.

"That's not a crime."

"It is if it spreads."

He poured two fingers of bourbon and drank half of it before continuing.

"The crew needs to feel inevitable. Like we're not just one

of the Five—we're the spine of the city."

"And Frankie?"

"He's a rib. Not the heart. But break enough ribs…"

"And the whole body stops breathing."

Salvatore finished the drink.

"I'll give him time. But not too much."

A red-brick warehouse in Tampa buzzed with new traffic. Crates offloaded under the cover of midnight humidity. Inside, two local contractors—Rudy Lang and Thomas Hines—counted stacks of liquor and paperwork.

One of them whistled low. "Hell of an operation for some Yanks."

The other nodded. "Hell of a lot of risk."

They turned as Luther Clay entered, coat slung over his shoulder, sweat darkening the collar of his shirt.

"This ain't a negotiation anymore," Luther said. "It's a route. And routes get protected."

The men exchanged glances again—this time with less hesitation.

Luther set a briefcase down on the table.

Ten thousand in clean bills.

"To help with comfort," he said. "And blindness."

Antonio Russo read the report through a monocle, brow furrowed in the study of his estate.

"Vitali just bought a harbor lot in Key West."

His consigliere raised a brow. "Was that part of the agreement?"

"No," Russo said. "It's a flank."

The consigliere remained still.

"Do we stop it?"

Antonio folded the paper.

"No. We *count* it. Every step. Every inch. Then we decide whether it's expansion…"

He exhaled slowly.

"Or encirclement."

Marco Lombardi read the same report in his own study.

He didn't curse.

He didn't smile.

He simply requested a message be sent.

"Get me someone in Frankie Romano's circle," he said.

"Anyone uncertain."

Part III - Two Nights Later - Carroll Street, Brooklyn

The diner was the kind that never closed, never updated its paint, and never asked too many questions. Frankie Romano sat alone in the back booth, the red vinyl seat cracked beneath him, his coffee going cold while he stirred it without drinking.

He hadn't slept.

Not really.

Ever since that conversation with Salvatore, his brain wouldn't stop spinning. Something in the boss's voice had changed—not threatening, but heavy. Final.

Frankie wasn't a coward. But he'd seen what happened to men who hesitated near power. And lately, everything about the crew—the ports, the warehouses, the trucks—they were moving faster than the ground beneath them.

And now someone had reached out.

He hadn't seen a face. Just a message.

"Let's talk. For everyone's good. 9 PM. Carroll Street."

No name. No family.

But he knew.

Lombardi.

He'd half-considered walking away. Just vanish. Ride the rails down to Philly or Baltimore. Start over as a mechanic or a janitor. Anything quiet.

But that wasn't how this ended.

So he waited.

At 9:12 PM, a man slid into the booth across from him. Gray suit. No tie. Face like a banker, eyes like a butcher.

"You're Frankie Romano," the man said.

Frankie didn't respond.

"We know you're unhappy. Rushed. Overworked. Forgotten. Vitali's a smart man, but he leaves behind the men who built him. It's not personal. It's just math."

Still, Frankie said nothing.

"We're not asking you to betray him. Just… keep your ears open. Tell us if he pushes too far. Or if someone else gets too bold."

Frankie stared at his coffee.

"You askin' me to be a rat?"

The man shook his head, calm.

"No. We're asking you to be smart. Alive. Men who do that tend to retire in warm places."

He slid an envelope across the table.

Frankie didn't touch it.

The man stood. "You don't have to say yes. But don't say no too loudly. Just think about it."

Then he was gone.

And Frankie was alone again.

Salvatore stood in the kitchen the next morning with Rosa, slicing fruit like it was strategy. Rico paced near the window, chewing the edge of his thumbnail.

"We sure it was Frankie?" Rico asked.

Claudia, seated with a stack of notes, nodded. "Lombardi sent a man. Quiet, but not quiet enough. We had eyes nearby. It wasn't a hit. It was a test."

"Frankie take the money?"

"No."

Salvatore placed the knife down.

"No hesitation?"

Claudia shook her head. "He didn't touch the envelope."

Rico exhaled hard. "So what? We pat him on the back and hope the next guy does the same?"

Salvatore looked at him.

"No," he said. "We remind him why he never needed to take it in the first place."

Frankie arrived late to the Cold House.

Salvatore was waiting at the same table, same chair, alone this time.

Frankie stepped in like a man walking into court.

"You know," he said.

Salvatore nodded. "I do."

Frankie stayed standing. "I didn't take it."

"I know."

"You think I wanted to?"

"I don't care what you wanted," Salvatore said. "Only what

you chose."

Frankie sat slowly.

Salvatore poured two drinks. Pushed one forward.

Frankie stared at it like it might be poison. Then drank.

Salvatore leaned back.

"You're not here because I don't trust you. You're here because I need you to understand what happens next."

Frankie waited.

"This family is getting bigger. Smarter. Stronger. That makes it harder to hold. The cracks won't come from bullets. They'll come from silence. From men thinking no one sees them fidget."

"I'm not fidgeting."

"No," Salvatore agreed. "You're worried. And you're not wrong to be."

Frankie lowered his eyes.

"I just… I didn't want to be the guy who tips the whole thing over."

"You won't," Salvatore said. "Because now you understand something the others don't."

Frankie raised an eyebrow. "What's that?"

Salvatore smiled, small and sharp.

"You're not just one of the crew anymore. You're one of the bones."

Frankie blinked.

"You're promoting me?"

Salvatore nodded.

"You'll oversee three of the new routes. Answer only to Luther and me. You'll meet the Tampa men next week."

Frankie leaned back, stunned.

"But… why?"

"Because you didn't take the envelope," Salvatore said. "And because if they ask again, I want them to realize they didn't just fail to turn you."

He leaned in.

"I want them to realize they made you *loyal*."

Frankie arrived in Tampa later that week with a trimmed beard, a clean coat, and a binder full of new manifests. He shook hands with Mason and Lang like he'd never doubted a single order. He laughed at their jokes. He asked about their kids. He adjusted shipping schedules before they realized the first one was wrong.

By the end of the meeting, they asked when he was coming back.

He told them, "Soon."

And meant it.

Marco Lombardi received the report just after lunch.

Romano didn't bite.

The man he'd sent across the table didn't get a second meeting.

Marco said nothing at first.

Then, calmly: "That's three."

His consigliere looked confused. "Three?"

Marco nodded. "Three men Vitali turned *loyal* by doing *nothing*."

He poured himself a drink.

"He's not just building routes. He's building *believers*."

A long pause.

Then the consigliere asked, "So what do we do?"

Marco sipped his drink and smiled.

"I still have one card to play; call Russo."

11

Rats in the Cellar

Part I - October, 1925 – Sullivan Street Flat, Early Morning

It started with the wrong questions being asked in the wrong rooms.

A Tampa shipment rerouted before it even left the rail yard.

A customs inspector suddenly "sick" two days after taking Vitali money.

Two Russo men spotted on the Jersey docks twenty minutes before a shipment was stolen—and twenty minutes after a route that only three of Salvatore's crew had access to was changed.

Coincidences didn't exist in Salvatore Vitali's world.

Not anymore.

He stood at the kitchen window, black coffee untouched, watching a cab idle too long across the street.

"They're moving faster," Rosa said from behind him, arms crossed.

"They're moving smarter," Salvatore corrected. "Which means someone's telling them how."

Rosa approached. "You know who?"

He shook his head. "Not yet."

She placed her hand on his shoulder. "You will."

He didn't say thank you.

He just stared harder.

The warehouse was full, and the crew was tense. They met at the Cold House that night.

Luther Clay ran inventory with a clipboard like it was a weapon. Claudia Voss stood near the chalkboard map, watching for patterns in chaos. Rico paced beside the door, fingers twitching toward his coat every time someone raised their voice.

Frankie Romano, back from Tampa, looked tired but calm. He watched the room more than the paperwork.

Salvatore stood at the center of the table. He didn't raise his voice.

"We had a leak," he said.

The room froze.

"No one's being accused," he continued. "Yet. But someone fed the Russos a route out of Key West. Three days ago."

A beat of silence.

Then murmurs.

Salvatore raised a hand.

"We're going to find out who. Quietly. Efficiently. And without warning. Rico will take half the crew, work backward from the manifests. Luther will audit the payment trail. Claudia—check communications. Every call, every errand. Even my own."

Claudia nodded without flinching.

"And me?" Frankie asked.

"You stick close to the warehouse. Keep things running smooth. If this mole is smart, they'll keep moving like nothing happened. That's how we catch them."

Frankie nodded.

Luther looked up from his clipboard. "You think it's one of ours?"

"I know it is," Salvatore said. "Because only one of ours knew that route changed."

Meanwhile, Antonio Russo read the list with shaking fingers at his estate, his left hand twitching from age or guilt. The names weren't valuable on their own. The patterns were.

"You're sure it's coming from the inside?" he asked.

His consigliere nodded.

"Then we protect the pipeline," Russo muttered. "Don't squeeze it. Let it keep flowing."

"But eventually he'll notice."

"Then we pray he finds the wrong man first."

Rico and Claudia returned to the flat that night, soaked from the rain, grim with discovery.

Salvatore met them in the front room.

"We found something," Claudia said, handing over a slip of paper. "One of the runners, Joey Triscari—he's been sending duplicate manifests."

Salvatore frowned. "Triscari's not high enough to know rail routes."

"He's not," Rico said. "But he's close to someone who is."

They exchanged a look.

"Vince Serra," Claudia said. "He's been coordinating manifests for the past month. Got bumped up after Massimo shifted south."

Salvatore processed it quickly. Vince Serra. Twenty-eight. Quiet. Loyal—but only outwardly. Hadn't asked for a raise. Hadn't missed a shift. Hadn't made a mistake.

Which made him perfect.

"Where is he now?" Salvatore asked.

Rico hesitated.

"Working the overnight manifest desk at the East Yard."

Salvatore reached for his coat.

"Then let's pay him a visit."

The East Yards office smelled like oil, sweat, and stale coffee. It was precisely 1:07 A.M. in Brooklyn.

Vince Serra sat hunched over a typewriter, pecking out forms like they meant something. He looked up as the door opened—and froze.

Salvatore. Rico. Silent. Present. Heavy.

"Boss," Vince said, standing too fast. "Didn't expect—"

"Sit," Salvatore said.

Vince did.

"You've been with us four years," Salvatore said, voice low. "Always showed up. Never rocked the boat."

"Yes, sir."

"Which is why I'm going to ask you this once."

Salvatore took a step closer.

"Did you feed the Russos our manifest?"

Vince blinked.

"No."

No hesitation.

No fear.

Which was the problem.

Salvatore turned to Rico.

"Pull his desk."

Rico started opening drawers. Then the cabinet. Then the wastebasket.

Finally, behind a loose wall panel: a stack of thin envelopes, each bearing dates, routes, and a small insignia used only by Russo's paper handlers.

Salvatore held one up.

"Still no?"

Vince swallowed.

"I—I was told it wasn't a problem. That it wouldn't go far."

"Who told you?"

Vince hesitated now.

Salvatore didn't ask twice.

He raised the envelope.

Rico didn't need a nod. Just a look.

One punch to the stomach. Then a backhand across the jaw. Vince dropped to his knees.

"Name," Salvatore said.

Vince gasped.

"Mr. Russo," he wheezed. "He promised money. A job in Jersey if things went south. He said it wasn't betrayal, it was... insurance."

Salvatore crouched down beside him.

"You think you were the first?"

Vince shook his head, eyes glistening. "Please—"

Salvatore stood.

"Rico."

But he raised a hand before Rico could draw his gun.

"No blood," Salvatore said. "Not here."

Vince exhaled—relief, fragile and thin.

"You'll live," Salvatore said. "But you'll vanish. Tonight. Quietly. You show your face again, even in Jersey, and I'll forget I spared you."

Vince nodded, dazed.

Rico spat on the floor. "Coward."

"No," Salvatore said. "A lesson."

Rosa read the ledger in silence later that morning.

"You found the leak."

Salvatore nodded.

"And you let him live?"

"Yes."

"Why?"

Salvatore poured a drink, then answered.

"Because next time Russo tries to recruit from the inside, he'll have to wonder who's already failed."

She looked up.

"And the crew?"

"I'll tell them the leak's plugged. But not who it was."

"Why not?"

Salvatore smiled faintly.

"Because fear doesn't just come from punishment."

He sipped his drink.

"It comes from not knowing how close they were to being next."

Part II - Next Morning - Eden Speakeasy, Backroom

The crew gathered under low lights and lower voices.

Gio Ferrara slumped in a chair, cigarette burning untouched between his fingers. Claudia Voss stood near the bar, arms folded tight. Luther Clay reviewed ledger notes, his jaw locked. Frankie Romano sipped coffee without sugar, staring at the grain of the table like it had secrets to give up.

Salvatore entered, coat still damp from the rain, and moved to the head of the table.

He didn't sit.

"There was a leak," he said.

No gasps. No murmurs. Just stillness.

"It's been sealed."

Gio finally spoke. "Who? Vince?"

"It doesn't matter."

"It matters to me," Gio snapped. "If we don't know who bled, how do we know who still has the knife?"

Salvatore met his gaze. "Because I said it's done."

Gio tensed but backed down.

Luther looked up. "You didn't kill him."

"No."

"Why?"

Salvatore scanned the room.

"Because fear is a currency. But trust is the vault that holds it. You kill every man who doubts, you teach the others to hide their fear. But you let one live, and they learn to *carry* it."

Frankie raised an eyebrow. "You think that lesson's enough?"

Salvatore nodded once. "I think it will echo."

Claudia stepped forward. "You want me to spread a version

of it?"

"Yes," Salvatore said. "Make it sound worse than it was. Say I broke his hands. Say he begged. Say his own mother doesn't recognize him."

Luther smiled. "Fear and myth, huh?"

Salvatore allowed a small grin.

"The city runs on both."

Frankie walked the length of the new intake corridor at the Red Hook Warehouse, clipboard in hand, calling out discrepancies as workers hustled past. Everything was back to normal, but normal had new weight to it now.

He turned as Rico approached.

"You believe it's over?" Frankie asked.

Rico shrugged. "Boss says it is."

"And you believe *him*?"

"I don't need to," Rico said. "I just know he wouldn't have let that guy walk if it didn't help the long game."

Frankie nodded slowly. "Still. Makes you think, doesn't it? About where the next crack comes from?"

"Yeah," Rico said. "And when it does, I hope it ain't us."

They stood in silence for a beat longer than necessary.

Then: "You sticking around this afternoon?" Frankie asked.

Rico nodded. "Boss wants everyone close. Just in case someone mistakes quiet for weakness."

Antonio Russo lit a cigar and read the latest update from his man inside the customs office later that night at his club in Midtown. No mention of Vince Serra. No footprint. No sign.

"Gone," he muttered.

His consigliere shifted in his seat. "That's not necessarily bad."

"No?" Russo hissed. "Then where's our next report? Where's our follow-up?"

The consigliere didn't answer.

"He found the leak," Russo said. "And he didn't kill him. Which means now *I* have to wonder if Vince talks."

"Vince is scared," the consigliere said. "He won't come back to New York."

"We have to move," Russo muttered. "We showed Vitali we can touch him, now we touch."

Rosa sat on the sofa that night, almost midnight, with a novel open in her lap, unread for the last hour.

"You've changed," she said finally.

Salvatore was still in his study, half-shadowed by the desk lamp.

"Have I?"

"You used to punish disloyalty with silence or steel."

"I still do," he said.

"No. Now you punish with doubt."

He looked at her.

"And that frightens you?"

She closed the book.

"It frightens me that it works."

He stood, crossed the room, sat beside her.

"This city is made of wolves," he said. "I used to think I had to out-howl them. Now I know I just need to remind them I *hear* better."

She placed her hand over his.

"And if one day they come in a pack?"

Salvatore didn't blink.

"Then I light a match and show them I'm willing to burn the forest down with us in it."

A few days later, Claudia's whisper campaign had taken root.

Bartenders were repeating it to dancers. Drivers were murmuring it to smugglers. Even a crew lieutenant in the Mancini operation had asked whether it was true that Salvatore tied a man to a boiler and left him alive just long enough to scream.

It wasn't true.

But it was useful.

Salvatore listened to the updates with a cool expression as Claudia laid them out.

"They're afraid to test you again. At least not directly."

"Good," Salvatore said. "Because I don't want them afraid of *me*."

Claudia raised an eyebrow.

"No?"

"I want them afraid of *what I'll become* when they force my hand."

Rico joined Salvatore near the edge of the Warehouse roof, both men smoking in silence as the city moved below them like a beast with too many eyes.

"You think he'll resurface?" Rico asked.

"Vince?"

Rico nodded.

"No," Salvatore said. "He knows I gave him one breath. That's all he'll get."

Rico exhaled. "We're lucky no one else followed him."

"We're not lucky," Salvatore said. "We're *early*. The cracks are coming. But now we've fortified."

He flicked ash off the roof ledge.

"And when they do come?"

Salvatore smiled.

"We'll hear the wood creak before it splinters."

Part III - Three Days Later - Red Hook, 3:14 A.M.

The first explosion was small—just enough to shatter glass and send rats screaming from their nests. The second came thirty seconds later, a controlled blaze that shot through the floor joists of the Vitali warehouse at Pier 18.

By the time the third went off, the sky was already glowing orange, and flames were licking across crates marked with shipping codes that had taken months to perfect.

Within ten minutes, half the structure was engulfed.

By twenty, it was gone.

No one died.

That wasn't the point.

The point was that someone had touched Salvatore Vitali's empire.

And they hadn't done it quietly.

Two hours later, Rico's voice crackled through the Sullivan Street flat hallway like gravel and lightning.

"It's gone, Sal. The whole pier. Shipping manifests, front crates, half a shipment from Tampa—all ash."

Salvatore sat at the kitchen table, dressed in a dark shirt, no tie. His hair was damp, like he'd woken from a storm.

"Casualties?"

"None. But the message was clear."

Salvatore stood, walked to the window, and stared into the gray sky.

"Russo?"

Rico didn't answer.

He didn't need to.

Claudia entered a moment later, slipping off her coat, face pale from smoke and morning whiskey.

"They used accelerants," she said. "Professional, not random. Two men seen near the pier an hour before. One's tied to Russo's payroll. I've already sent his picture to Luther."

Salvatore nodded.

"Don't kill him," he said.

Claudia blinked. "Not even a finger?"

"No," he said. "Let him run."

Rico frowned. "Why?"

"Because Russo thinks we're still playing by the old rules. He lights a fire. I draw a line. He gets to choose where the next match falls."

Rosa appeared in the doorway.

"Then draw the line," she said.

Salvatore turned to her, calm despite the storm behind his eyes.

"Oh, I will."

The crew assembled under hush and tension a the Eden. No jokes today. No music from the next room. The smell of ash still clung to their coats.

Frankie leaned forward. "We rebuilding the pier?"

"Eventually," Salvatore said. "But first, we remind them

we're not *there* anymore. We're everywhere."

Luther pulled out a map. "Our real volume's running through Jersey now. Tampa's untouched. Clay's boys rerouted a shipment through Key West last night before the fire even started."

Claudia added, "Russo hit a memory, not a nerve. We lost paper, not power."

Gio didn't look convinced. "Still. People talk. They'll say Russo hit you and you didn't hit back."

Salvatore smiled. "Then let them say it."

"Until?" Gio asked.

"Until they see the fire wasn't meant for *me*," Salvatore replied. "It was a flare. A signal. And now I know exactly who wants the smoke."

Antonio Russo stood in front of the fireplace, swirling brandy in a crystal glass, the flames reflecting off his eyes.

"You think he'll retaliate?" his consigliere asked.

Russo didn't answer at first. He simply stared at the flames.

"He won't strike back," Russo said finally. "Not yet. He's too careful. Too calculated. He'll twist it. Use it."

The consigliere folded his arms. "And if you're wrong?"

Russo smiled thinly.

"Then we watch something beautiful burn."

Salvatore stood on the edge of the ruined pier.

Cinders blew across his shoes. The water hissed as embers dropped into the tide. Men moved around him, cleaning, rebuilding, pretending this was just another setback.

But he wasn't watching the wreckage.

He was watching the skyline.

The city had blinked.
And next time, it would *bow*.

12

Mancini's Ultimatum

Part I - November, 1925 – Midtown, The Waldorf Room

The chandelier above the circular table flickered once—a stutter of light that passed unnoticed by the waitstaff but not by the men below it.

Salvatore Vitali entered the room five minutes late.

Not out of arrogance.

Out of clarity.

Every man at the table watched him with a different temperature behind their eyes.

Antonio Russo was unusually quiet. A red silk scarf hid the tremble in his throat, but his eyes darted like a man who knew his fire had ignited more than a warehouse.

Marco Lombardi leaned back with his arms crossed, studying Salvatore like a puzzle that refused to be solved.

Vincent DeMarco's chair remained empty—again.

And at the head, as always, sat Carlo Mancini, the man who'd once kept peace by sheer force of presence. Today, he looked tired. Elegant in his double-breasted gray suit, but weary in a way that even his diamond cufflinks couldn't hide.

"Salvatore," Carlo said as the young don took his seat. "Thank you for joining us."

The words were polite.

The tone was not.

Salvatore nodded once. "My apologies. I was seeing to reconstruction."

"A warehouse?" Marco asked, feigning innocence. "Heard it was quite the blaze."

"It was," Salvatore replied. "But our business moves faster than fire."

Russo shifted uncomfortably. Carlo raised a hand.

"That's exactly the problem," he said. "Your business. Your movement. Your influence."

Salvatore folded his hands on the table.

"I assumed that was the goal. Stability through strength."

Carlo leaned forward. "There's a difference between strength and sovereignty."

The room went still.

Salvatore didn't blink.

"Are you accusing me of something, Carlo?"

"I'm not accusing," Mancini said. "I'm warning."

He stood, voice low and deliberate.

"You've built fast. Smart. But too far. Too loud. You've retaliated in whispers when blood demanded thunder. And now half the city whispers you hold the strings that once belonged to all of us."

Salvatore said nothing.

Carlo circled the table slowly.

"There must be order. Balance. For decades, we've survived because no one dared call themselves king."

He stopped behind Salvatore's chair.

"I won't allow another boss of bosses to rise."

Salvatore turned slightly in his seat.

"I never called myself king."

"No," Carlo said. "But others have. And your silence lets it echo."

Russo finally found his voice. "You could stop this. Bend the knee. Clarify the structure."

"Structure," Salvatore repeated, flatly.

Carlo stepped forward.

"You'll pledge fealty to this table, this commission. And to me, as arbiter and tie-breaker. Or you'll face consequences."

Marco looked up, amused. "Consequences like what, Carlo?"

Carlo ignored him.

His eyes stayed locked on Salvatore.

"You'll declare your loyalty here, now. Or you'll leave this table for good."

Salvatore stood.

Slowly. Smoothly.

And when he spoke, his voice was calm, but iron underneath.

"I came here because I believed in the value of five voices guiding this city. Not one voice in an empty room with a louder echo."

He stepped away from the chair.

"I respected you, Carlo. Still do. But I won't kneel to a man who sees strength as threat and silence as disloyalty."

Carlo's hand twitched near his pocket.

Marco stood as well, casually.

"Easy, gentlemen," he said. "Let's not make today a day of memory."

Salvatore adjusted his coat.

"Today is a day of memory," he said. "Because years from now, everyone at this table will remember it as the moment things changed."

He looked at Carlo.

"You want kings? You'll get wars. You want peace? Then stop asking lions to kneel like lambs."

And then he left.

Just like that.

Rico slammed the door shut behind him at the flat.

"You should've shot him."

Salvatore poured himself a drink.

"That's why I'm at the table," he said. "Because I don't shoot until the moment matters."

Rosa watched from the doorway, arms folded.

"You think Carlo's done talking?"

"No," Salvatore said. "I think he's already moving."

Claudia entered from the kitchen, coat still on.

"Lombardi's staying neutral for now. But Russo's rattling cages. DeMarco's men are taking bets on whether you'll survive the month."

Salvatore took a slow sip of bourbon.

"I always liked being the underdog."

Frankie leaned against the hallway wall, voice low.

"What now?"

Salvatore set his glass down.

"Now we prepare."

"For what?"

Salvatore looked up, the weight of inevitability in his gaze.

"For the day Carlo Mancini finds out what happens when the lion doesn't roar."

Part II - Two Days Later - Midtown, The Garden at Eden

Rain whispered against the windows, soft and constant. Inside, Eden's VIP lounge buzzed with the low hum of cigar smoke, whispered numbers, and men too careful to admit which way they were leaning.

Salvatore Vitali sat at the table in the back, glass of Chianti untouched, ledger open beside him.

Opposite him sat Alfonso Greco, one of Mancini's top lieutenants, known for his steady temperament and his impeccable memory. Greco had handled most of the Mancini union rackets along the Brooklyn docks for over a decade.

He was loyal.

But not necessarily blind.

"You realize what you're asking," Greco said, his voice gravel wrapped in silk. "Carlo raised me. Brought me in when I had holes in my shoes and two dead brothers."

"I'm not asking for betrayal," Salvatore said. "I'm offering survival."

Greco leaned back. "You think this turns bloody?"

"I think it already has," Salvatore said. "Russo burned my warehouse. Carlo demanded a throne. That wasn't a request—it was a warning. He's afraid."

Greco frowned. "Of what?"

"Of irrelevance," Salvatore answered. "And men who rule out of fear die fearing everything."

Greco glanced at the room's edge, where Claudia Voss leaned near the bar, making no effort to hide her listening.

"You always surround yourself with wolves?"

"I feed them," Salvatore replied. "That's why they don't bite."

Greco tapped the table with one thick finger.

"You want my backing. That means I shift the docks. The union hands. Two captains who owe me favors."

Salvatore nodded.

"You get them. Quietly. And I protect you when this thing turns. Not just from Carlo. From everyone."

Greco's eyes narrowed.

"And if it doesn't turn?"

Salvatore finally lifted his glass.

"Then we both burn. But I'm the only one who planned for the fire."

They drank.

And the first brick of Carlo's wall began to fall.

Marco Lombardi read the early reports with a growing sense of amusement at his estate.

"Greco?"

His consigliere nodded. "He met with Vitali two nights ago. Started pulling his men off Mancini operations yesterday."

Marco laughed once, short, surprised.

"I always thought it would be Russo who had lit the match. Turns out Carlo handed Vitali the torch himself."

His consigliere remained silent.

Marco stood, stretched, paced toward the large window facing the sea.

"Let them weaken each other. I'll inherit the ashes."

They met at the flat, in the kitchen. The crew gathered in tighter formation these days. No more idle jokes. No more late-night poker. Something about Carlo's ultimatum had made everything sharper.

Frankie Romano spoke first. "Greco's turning?"

"He's softening," Salvatore said. "I gave him two routes, a promise of autonomy, and protection when the storm hits."

Luther Clay snorted. "You think Carlo won't see that coming?"

"I'm counting on it," Salvatore replied. "Let him lash out. Let him show the others how small his empire really is."

Claudia sat back. "And if Carlo moves first?"

"Then he's predictable," Salvatore said. "And when a king becomes predictable, he becomes replaceable."

Gio Ferrara drummed his fingers on the table.

"You planning to replace him?"

Salvatore looked at him, steady, unreadable.

"I'm planning to make the crown unnecessary."

Carlo Mancini stared across his table in Little Italy at a trembling captain named Arturo Bellini, whose voice cracked with each sentence.

"They're moving, boss. Quietly. Greco's handing out envelopes with Vitali's seal. Two of the dock reps from Red Hook haven't checked in for days."

Carlo didn't speak.

Didn't blink.

He simply poured himself a glass of grappa and drank it slowly.

When he spoke, his voice was low and quiet—quieter than Arturo wanted.

"You know what your problem is, Bellini?"

Bellini swallowed hard.

"You think men like Vitali change the game by brute force. They don't. They change it by talking to men like you—men who'd rather survive a little longer than go down with the ship."

Bellini opened his mouth.

Carlo held up a hand.

"Next time you bring me bad news, make sure you're not part of it."

Bellini nodded, pale and sweating.

"Get out."

Greco returned to the Eden that night with a folded map and a list of names.

"These are the captains willing to shift—no questions asked," he said. "But if Carlo moves now, they'll run."

"Then we move first," Salvatore said. "Give them proof."

"Of what?"

"That we're already in control."

Claudia leaned forward. "You want a strike?"

"No," Salvatore said. "I want a transfer."

He tapped the map.

"This warehouse used to be Mancini's. Bought under one of Carlo's holding companies, but the paperwork's old. Luther's cousin found a clause in the lease. If no activity's recorded for ninety days, the property reverts to city ownership."

Frankie blinked. "That's this month."

"Exactly," Salvatore said. "We take it legally. No blood. No flames. And we fill it by sunrise."

Greco chuckled. "You're not trying to win a war. You're trying to buy the city while they're still counting bullets."

Salvatore raised his glass again.

"And so far, it's cheaper."

Carlo sat in his study, papers scattered across his desk, news reports beside copies of ledgers once full of Mancini assets.

Gone. Acquired. Co-opted.

Piece by piece, Salvatore wasn't attacking.

He was absorbing.

Carlo's consigliere entered, quiet, nervous.

"What do you want to do?"

Carlo didn't look up.

"Send word to the Vitali Outfit," he said.

The consigliere hesitated.

"Another meeting?"

Carlo finally looked up.

"No. This isn't a meeting."

He paused, voice thin and sharp.

"This is a warning."

Part III - Three Nights Later - Upper West Side, Private Hall Above Da Romano's

The lights were dimmed for effect, not ambiance. The long oak table stretched beneath an antique chandelier, flickering as if unsure whether to fully illuminate what was happening.

Carlo Mancini stood at the head of the table. Alone. No advisors, no soldiers.

Across from him sat Salvatore Vitali.

This time, they didn't bother inviting the rest of the Five. No need.

They both knew this wasn't diplomacy.

It was declaration.

"I gave you respect," Carlo said, voice steady. "I gave you a seat, Salvatore. I gave you legitimacy."

"You gave me conditions," Salvatore replied. "Legitimacy was something I earned."

Carlo's lips thinned.

"I could have crushed you before the second pier was built. Before you reached Tampa. Before the unions started calling you instead of me."

"But you didn't," Salvatore said. "Because part of you wanted to see if I could do what you never could—build something without starting a war."

Carlo leaned forward. "You're building a bomb. Everyone sees it. They're just waiting for it to go off."

Salvatore didn't blink.

"Then they'd better decide quickly which side of the blast they want to be on."

A long silence stretched between them.

Then Carlo spoke again, quieter now.

"You bend the knee, Salvatore. One last time. You take the table names with yours—one commission, with me as the chair—and this ends here. No more warehouses lost. No more whispers in the dark. You keep your empire. But it belongs to *us*."

Salvatore stood slowly.

"I already said my answer."

"Then say it again."

Salvatore met his eyes.

"I don't kneel."

He turned and walked to the door.

Carlo's voice followed him.

"You're going to regret this."

Salvatore paused with his hand on the doorknob.

"I already do," he said. "Because this city deserved to be ruled by wisdom. But now it will settle for *memory*."

And then he was gone.

Rain hit the windows like gravel at the flat. Salvatore stood in the study, tie loosened, shirt sleeves rolled up. Rosa poured him a drink without asking.

"You're done talking," she said.

"Yes."

"Then it begins."

He didn't argue.

Frankie entered quietly with Claudia behind him.

Claudia handed over a sealed envelope.

"Greco's move is final. The docks are ours. The Longshore union voted this afternoon. All transport goes through Vitali channels now."

"Any blowback?"

"Only silence," Claudia said. "Which is worse."

Rico came in next, trench coat still wet.

"Russo's got a meet scheduled in Red Hook tomorrow. A warehouse *we* used to use. His nephew, two of his captains, maybe even Antonio himself. They're planning something."

Salvatore turned to him.

"How many guards?"

"Minimal. He's gotten cocky. Thinks the fire gave him space."

Salvatore sat at the desk.

"No more silence. No more waiting."

He looked up.

"We hit them."

Frankie raised an eyebrow. "How hard?"

Salvatore's voice never rose.

"Enough to make sure Antonio Russo never speaks again."

Salvatore sat with Rosa beside him, drink in hand, ledger on the desk in the Eden's private office.

"We took the docks," Rosa said. "We took Tampa. We even took Russo's silence."

"And Carlo?" she asked.

Salvatore leaned back.

"We let him watch."

She frowned. "You're not going to finish it?"

"No," he said. "He needs to *see* what he failed to contain. He needs to feel every breath I take as a reminder he lost the throne before he even knew he sat on it."

Rico entered with a grin.

"Got news."

Salvatore looked up.

"The other families are already backing off the docks. Lombardi sent word—neutrality reaffirmed. DeMarco's enforcers haven't moved in two days."

Salvatore nodded.

"It's done."

Claudia lit a cigarette at the window.

"For now," she said.

Salvatore smiled, slow and sharp.

"Now for the show. "

13

The Warehouse Massacre

Part I - November, 1925 - Brooklyn Industrial Corridor, 3:28 A.M.

The warehouse squatted between two rusting rail lines like a bloated corpse—ugly, forgotten, and thriving in its anonymity.

Inside, the Russo crew buzzed like hornets. Wooden crates were stacked in rows, each marked with false union stamps and stuffed with Cuban rum, stolen weapons, and enough cash to bribe a dozen city officials.

Carlo Russo, nephew to the old man himself, leaned against a crate near the center of the loading floor. He was younger than the others—slick, gold chain, new shoes—and had the kind of grin only men born into power wore.

Beside him stood Dominic Vizzini, one of Russo's few trusted lieutenants still drawing breath. He pointed at a manifest sheet.

"Second shipment's delayed. We push it through Jersey tomorrow."

Carlo shrugged. "We got more coming. Let 'em wait."

Vizzini raised an eyebrow. "You think Vitali's really done? He hasn't moved since the warehouse fire. Not one shot."

"That's how I know he's done," Carlo smirked. "He knows who runs this city now."

Vizzini opened his mouth to reply—

—and the world split open.

The first explosion tore through the southwest wall like a shotgun through wet paper, hurling steel and shrapnel into the air. A second blast, hidden beneath a stack of Russo crates, sent fire licking the rafters.

Men screamed. Wood splintered. A forklift flipped like a matchbox.

Then came the third.

A charge planted under the center of the warehouse floor erupted in a thunderclap that sent crates, bodies, and concrete into the sky. Flame billowed out in all directions, devouring everything in its reach.

By 3:33 A.M., the entire structure was gone.

The air stank of fuel, blood, and the charred remains of over a dozen Russo men.

Including Carlo Russo and Dominic Vizzini.

The fire hadn't even reached the morning papers.

But Salvatore Vitali already knew as he sat in his study.

Claudia handed him a telegram: six lines, no names, just two words repeated.

Ash fell. Ash rose.

Salvatore folded it and slipped it into the fire.

Frankie stood by the window, stunned. "That was half their senior crew. One more blast and there's no Russo family left to bury."

"We don't need one more," Salvatore said. "We needed *this* one."

Rico stepped in from the hallway. "They'll come for us now. No more business. No more rules."

"They were never following the rules," Salvatore said calmly. "They lit the fire. We just turned it into light."

Rosa emerged from the hall, tying her robe.

"You started a war."

"No," Salvatore said. "I ended a hesitation."

Carlo Mancini stood by the railing of the Brooklyn Bridge, coat buttoned to his throat, eyes fixed on the black smoke rising in the distance.

"That was a message," he said to his driver. "No accident. No random."

Behind him, Marco Lombardi stepped out of a second car.

"You hear who got hit?"

Carlo nodded. "Russo's heir. Vizzini. Seven lieutenants. Three transport men. One bookkeeper."

Marco whistled. "He's not just making moves anymore. He's drawing *maps*."

Carlo didn't speak.

He just stared at the smoke until it drifted out of sight.

The DeMarco Safehouse was somber. The table was silent as news of the explosion rolled in.

Vincent DeMarco, pale and sunken, tapped a spoon against a glass without rhythm.

His consigliere, Matteo, leaned in. "What's the play, boss?"

Vincent's voice cracked with exhaustion.

"Call my nephew, Nico. Tell him I'm back in charge. Things have gotten interesting, and it looks like a new dog in the yard needs to be put in its place."

The crew assembled like iron filings to a magnet in the Eden speakeasy—Rico, Claudia, Frankie, Luther, Gio. None of them looked surprised. Only resolved.

Luther dropped a dossier on the table. "Fire crews called it a freak gas explosion. No one's talking. Not even their cousins."

Claudia followed up. "And the survivors? Two made it to hospitals. Cops are holding them. One's missing half his face."

Salvatore poured a drink. "No loose ends?"

"None that can speak," Rico said.

Frankie leaned in. "You just made yourself the most dangerous man in New York."

Salvatore smiled faintly.

"Good."

The Russo Social Club building stood quiet under the falling dusk. Inside, only two men remained: Franco Russo, Antonio's cousin, and Leo Romano, a childhood friend turned underboss.

They stared at the paper.

Explosion Kills 14 in Suspected Gang Violence.

Below it: a single line.

Sources point to retaliation.

Franco slammed his fist on the table.

"He wants war?"

"He *is* war," Leo muttered.

Franco stood. "Then we burn him. We go after his lieutenants. One by one."

Leo shook his head.

"No."

Franco froze.

"What?"

Leo stood too, slowly.

"We don't go after him. We *join* someone else."

Franco blinked.

"You're saying we flip?"

"I'm saying we survive."

Part II - Later That Night - Sullivan Street Flat

The fire had faded from the skyline, but not from memory.

Salvatore stood at the window, sleeves rolled up, smoke from his cigarette curling upward like a warning. He wasn't watching the street. He was watching the rhythm—cars that passed too slow, lights that flickered a second longer than usual. Movement out of place. Patterns breaking.

He could always tell when the rules were shifting.

Rico came in, setting a folder on the desk. "Damage was high. The two main lieutenants are confirmed dead. But a few made it out. Word is the family's regrouping, not retaliating."

"And the message?" Salvatore asked.

"Loud and clear. The Russos know they got hit for overstepping. They're falling back, not striking out."

Claudia entered next, her tone measured. "Franco Russo wants a meet. Private. Used the old signal code. The kind only sent when they're looking to keep their heads, not win a war."

Salvatore turned from the window.

"Neutral ground. Ten minutes. If it's a trap, we walk out slower than we walked in."

The lights were low. The room quiet at the Eden.

Franco Russo sat at the end of the long table, coat draped over the chair beside him, hands clasped—not in submission, but calculation.

Salvatore entered with Rico and Claudia in tow. He took the opposite seat without ceremony.

"You have five minutes," Salvatore said.

Franco nodded. "We know who set the fire. We know why you struck back."

"Do you?" Salvatore asked.

"You hit us hard, but not completely. You could've finished us. You didn't."

Salvatore remained still. "That was a courtesy. One time only."

Franco leaned in. "We want out of the fire. No retaliation. No escalation. We pull back to Queens and the Bronx—territories we know. You keep the waterfront and your southern line."

Rico narrowed his eyes. "And why should we believe you?"

"Because half my men are gone," Franco said, flatly. "Because Antonio's scorched earth plan got us burned. And because we're not here to win anymore. We're here to survive."

Salvatore considered him. Then nodded.

"You'll keep your space. But no shipments without notice. No foot soldiers outside your zones. And if another one of your men sets fire to anything I own—"

"It won't happen," Franco said quickly. "We'll keep our house quiet."

Salvatore stood. "Then keep it quiet. And next time someone in your bloodline wants a war, remind them what it sounds like when they lose the first battle."

Luther Clay walked the perimeter of Warehouse 16 in Red Hook with two lieutenants, clipboard in hand.

"We shift operations here. Russo's dock presence is neutralized, but not erased. They've still got street clout."

Frankie nodded. "You think they're really standing down?"

"For now," Luther said. "They've got broken bones. They're licking 'em. But they're not dead."

Gio approached with updates. "Mancini's watching. Carlo hasn't moved. But if he does—it won't be for Russo."

Frankie smirked. "He'll come for us."

Luther adjusted his hat. "Let him. We've already got the high ground."

Marco Lombardi poured a drink for Carlo Mancini at the estate in Staten Island, watching the older man as he absorbed the news.

"You hear Russo's pulling back?"

"I heard he got slapped," Carlo said. "And now he's bowing."

"He could've been wiped out."

"But he wasn't."

Carlo sipped his drink. "Vitali's not just ruthless. He's calculated. Keeps the game going. Doesn't break the board."

Marco smiled. "Maybe he's learned something from us after all."

Carlo's voice dropped. "Or maybe he's just biding time until he builds his own table."

Later that night, Rosa looked up from the day's ledgers. "You spared them."

Salvatore sat at the desk, calm as the rain against the windows.

"No. I offered them a choice. War or whisper."

"And they took whisper."

"For now."

Rico entered with a report. "Their crews are quiet. Even the ones who used to brag in bars. It's like they remember how loud the fire was."

Salvatore nodded. "Good. That's how it should be remembered."

Claudia joined Salvatore on the Eden rooftop, lighting a cigarette as they looked out over the lights of the city.

"You think they'll stay in their corner?" she asked.

"No," Salvatore said. "But I think the next time they step out of it, they'll ask permission first."

She exhaled slowly. "That's the best kind of victory. The kind no one can claim—but everyone obeys."

Salvatore smirked.

"We don't need to be kings. Just the men they count the shadows from."

Part III - Next Morning - Westchester, Mancini Estate

Carlo Mancini stared into the fireplace of his study. Logs cracked and hissed in front of him, but his eyes were focused far beyond the flames.

Behind him, his consigliere, Enzo Costa, paced silently. He had delivered the morning reports personally, not trusting messengers—not today.

"They met," Enzo said. "Franco and Salvatore. It was cordial. Conditional. No demands."

Carlo didn't move.

"No retaliation?" he finally asked.

"None. The Russos are backing off. Restructuring in Queens. Pulling their teeth from the docks."

"And Salvatore?"

"Untouched. Unchallenged."

Carlo exhaled through his nose. "So he strikes a match, burns part of a dynasty, and gets loyalty for the ash."

Enzo stopped pacing. "Some say it was strategic mercy."

"No," Carlo growled. "It was conquest dressed as courtesy."

He stood slowly, the weight of age on his spine, but not in his hands.

"He's bleeding the city one ally at a time. First Greco. Then the unions. Now Russo's silence. If I wait another week, I'll be kneeling just to keep my chair."

Enzo hesitated. "Then what do we do?"

Carlo turned.

"We remind him that silence isn't the same as surrender."

A quiet Vitali courier stepped through the alley behind the meat market in the Bronx, carrying an envelope marked with a single V.

He didn't see the man in the butcher's apron until it was too late.

A blade slid between his ribs—quick, efficient, personal.

No message. No note. Just the absence of one.

The Vitali envelope never reached its destination.

By nightfall, Claudia had counted three couriers missing, two storefronts shuttered under pressure, and one of their lower captains bruised and bloodied behind a deli in Arthur Avenue.

The Mancinis weren't striking hard.

They were striking *deep*.

Salvatore read the updated report in silence while the crew waited that night at the Eden.

Rico, Frankie, Claudia, Gio, and Luther—all present, all tense.

Three silent attacks. All surgically delivered. No civilians. No mess. Just the message.

"He's probing," Claudia said. "Testing to see if we blink."

Frankie looked ready to explode. "We should hit back. Hard. Right in Midtown. Let him choke on his own name."

"No," Salvatore said. "That's what he wants. A war he can justify."

Rico leaned forward. "Then what? We let him nip at us like a dog?"

"No," Salvatore said again. "We show him we're not dogs."

He stood and walked to the chalk map at the far end of the room.

"There's a Mancini-owned courier hub near Port Morris. He's using it to funnel messages and cash—off-grid. Untraceable."

Luther nodded. "We hit it?"

"We don't burn it. We take it."

Frankie frowned. "Isn't that escalation?"

Salvatore turned, eyes calm but unyielding.

"No. It's occupation."

Rosa watched Salvatore from the doorway of the flat, arms folded.

"Another war?"

He shook his head, removing his cufflinks.

"This isn't war. It's succession."

She stepped into the room. "So Carlo's the old king?"

"He is," Salvatore said. "But he doesn't know yet that the crown's already changed heads."

Rosa approached him slowly.

"And if he forces your hand?"

"Then he won't live long enough to see what I build after."

Carlo lit a cigar slowly in his clubhouse. The ritual mattered. Every motion measured. Every breath controlled.

Across from him sat Luca Greco. Alfonso's nephew. Young. Ambitious. Reckless.

"He's not retaliating," Luca said.

"Because he's calculating," Carlo replied. "That's what makes him dangerous."

"He's consolidating the port in Jersey now. That's DeMarco turf."

"I know," Carlo said. "And DeMarco won't stop him."

"You think he's scared?"

"No," Carlo said. "He's waiting to see who bleeds first."

Carlo looked up at Luca.

"I need you to make him bleed. Quietly. Subtly. Nothing flashy."

"What do you want hit?"

"Something *important*. But not irreplaceable."

Luca nodded and left without another word.

Carlo exhaled slowly, watching the smoke curl.

"You want a crown, Vitali?" he muttered. "Then wear it while the knives come."

Claudia joined Salvatore on the rooftop, handing over a slip of paper.

"Mancini moved three crews across the river. Luca Girono's boys. All eyes say they're looking for cracks."

Salvatore looked out at the city.

"It's not cracks they'll find."

"No?"

"It's teeth."

She lit a cigarette. "What's our next step?"

"We pull in the flanks. Lock down Brooklyn. Move Franco's intel into Lombardi zones without being obvious."

"And Mancini?"

Salvatore turned to her.

"We make him think he's still in control."

Claudia smiled faintly. "Until?"

"Until the day he gives an order and no one moves."

Salvatore's voice dropped.

"And that's when he'll understand—his shadow's already been sold."

14

Rosa's Plea

Part I - Winter, 1926 - Sullivan Street Flat

Snow fell in thick, silent sheets outside the window, muffling the city like a shroud. Streetlights flickered behind the glass, casting long shadows across the room where Rosa Vitali held her newborn son.

He was swaddled in white, blinking up at her with heavy eyes that hadn't yet chosen their color. She rocked slowly, humming a lullaby only she remembered.

Salvatore stood in the doorway.

Still.

Watching.

He had seen men die in alleys. Had watched empires burn from the inside. But nothing—nothing—had ever struck him silent like the sight of his wife cradling their child.

Rosa looked up and smiled softly. "He looks like you."

"He cries less," Salvatore replied.

She chuckled. "For now."

He stepped forward, cautiously, as if the baby were made of glass instead of flesh and fire.

"Joseph," Rosa said. "That's what I told the nurse."

Salvatore blinked. "A strong name."

" A name that stands."

Salvatore reached down, touched his son's hand. The fingers curled instinctively around one of his.

"Joseph Vitali," he said softly, and the name echoed in the silence like a promise.

Snow still covered the rooftops a few days later, but inside the speakeasy, heat poured from the walls in the form of energy and whispers.

Rico paced near the bar, reading the latest movement logs. Claudia spoke with one of their runners, handing off envelopes for the southern crews. Luther reviewed protection payments across Queens, now stabilized after Russo's quiet withdrawal.

Salvatore entered slowly, almost reluctantly.

Frankie was the first to see him. "Hey," he said. "You good?"

Salvatore gave a single nod. "I'm a father."

That stilled the room more than any gunshot.

Claudia blinked. "Boy or girl?"

"Boy."

"Strong?" Luther asked.

"Stronger than he knows," Salvatore said. "Rosa named him Joseph."

Rico grinned. "Another Vitali. Just what the city needed."

But Salvatore didn't smile.

He sat at the head of the table and looked at each of them in turn.

"I want this war to end."

Frankie scoffed. "We all do."

"No," Salvatore said firmly. "I mean it. No more expansions. No more territory for the sake of territory. From this point forward, we defend. We don't chase."

Claudia raised an eyebrow. "Since when did we start building walls instead of bridges?"

"Since I became a father," Salvatore replied. "I built an empire for legacy. Now I need to make sure it doesn't become a graveyard."

The room fell silent again.

Then Rico leaned in. "What's the plan?"

"We fortify," Salvatore said. "We consolidate. And when Carlo makes his next move, we end it. Not through politics. Not through leverage."

His voice dropped.

"We end it with finality."

Rosa sat near the fire later that night, Joseph sleeping beside her in a bassinet made by her grandmother's hands. She didn't look up when Salvatore entered.

"You meant it?" she asked.

"Yes."

"No more war?"

"One more," Salvatore said. "The last."

Rosa looked over. "Can you promise that?"

He didn't answer right away. Then: "No. But I can try."

She reached for his hand.

"You've built a world around fire and steel. If you want peace now, you'll have to smother every ember yourself."

"I will," he said. "For him."

Rosa nodded.

"Then let's hope he never has to understand what you became to give him peace."

Carlo Mancini stared out across the frozen gardens that surrounded his home, the same ones he had walked with diplomats, killers, and allies over the past thirty years.

He no longer walked them.

His legs had weakened, but not his pride.

Luca Greco stood nearby, arms folded, expression hard. "They're pulling back. Vitali hasn't expanded in three months. Not a foot of new territory. No new businesses. He's shifting to a defensive posture."

Carlo narrowed his eyes. "That's not peace. That's preparation."

"Maybe he's tired."

"No," Carlo said. "He's planting something. When a wolf stops moving, it's not because it's wounded. It's because it smells blood up ahead."

Luca leaned in. "You want us to strike?"

Carlo didn't reply.

But in his eyes, something colder than winter settled in.

Claudia joined Salvatore on the Eden roof, coat pulled tight, snowflakes catching in her dark hair.

"He's going to come for us," she said.

"I know."

"And you'll be ready?"

Salvatore looked toward the horizon.

"I'm always ready."

Claudia hesitated. "You think you'll really stop after this?"

"I have to," he said. "If I don't, then Joseph doesn't inherit a name—he inherits a target."

She nodded, then handed him a folded note.

"What's this?" he asked.

"Word from Sicily," Claudia said. "Someone from your father's time. They've arrived in the city."

Salvatore frowned, unfolding the paper.

A single name was written on it.

Marcelo Barone.

He stared at the name, then crumpled the note.

"Bury that," he said.

"But—"

"I said bury it."

Claudia hesitated.

Then nodded.

And the snow kept falling.

Part II - Two Days Later - The Garden at Eden

It was a quiet morning at Eden, unusually so. The snow outside still hadn't melted, and the city had taken on a soft silence that didn't match the tension creeping into the room.

Salvatore sat at the head of the table with Claudia at his left and Rico at his right. Neither spoke as the man entered.

Marcelo Barone.

Older than expected. Gray in the beard, still black in the eyes. Dressed like he'd never left Sicily—long wool coat, leather gloves, scarf worn like armor. His hands bore the marks of old labor, but his walk was still that of someone who knew where the blade was hidden in every room.

He didn't bow. Didn't smile. Just said:

"Salvatore."

"Barone," Salvatore replied.

"You look like your father."

"I'm not him."

Barone smiled faintly. "I know."

He took the seat opposite.

Claudia slid a folder across the table. "You arrived under another name. Why?"

Barone ignored her and kept his eyes on Salvatore.

"I came to speak with the one man in this city who understands what it costs to build something that lasts."

Salvatore didn't respond.

Barone continued. "You've made enemies of men your father would've bent to. You've made allies out of men who would've slit your throat for a dime ten years ago. That's not just survival. That's empire."

"I didn't build an empire," Salvatore said. "I built a future."

Barone nodded. "And that's why I'm here. Because your father never got that chance."

A long silence followed.

Rico leaned forward. "Get to the point."

Barone folded his gloved hands. "Before your father left Sicily, he wasn't just a soldier in a clan. He was a man with a blood debt. A murder. A betrayal. A brother buried in a field outside Palermo."

Salvatore's jaw tightened. "That's history."

"It's not," Barone said. "Because the son of that murdered man is coming to this city now. And he doesn't care about your titles, your turf, or your family. He just wants your blood."

Salvatore stood, slow and sharp. "You come into my house, uninvited, to tell me my son has a target on his back?"

"I came to tell you that you need me to stop him."

Claudia frowned. "And why would you help us?"

Barone looked at her, then at Salvatore.

"Because your father saved my life once. And because I'm the only man who knows how to find Adriano Ferri before he finds you."

Later that afternoon, Rosa held Joseph in her arms, swaying gently as snowflakes drifted past the window.

Salvatore stood by the doorway, hands still.

"He's growing fast," Rosa said.

"He's going to have to."

She looked up at him. "I heard you met the man from Sicily."

"Barone. My father's shadow."

"What does he want?"

"To clear a debt. Or collect one."

Rosa placed Joseph in his crib. "And this man chasing you—Adriano Ferri?"

Salvatore nodded.

"He wants to take what your father left behind."

"He wants to take what *I* built."

Rosa crossed the room. "Then promise me something."

Salvatore met her eyes.

"Promise me you'll stop him, and not end up like your father."

The crew gathered under soft light in the Eden safehouse.

Rico laid out the intel: Ferri had been tracked to Naples briefly, using an alias. Then silence. No hits on any federal logs, no connections through known networks.

"He's a ghost," Claudia said.

"No," Barone replied. "He's a storm. He waits for the moment no one sees him coming."

Frankie leaned against the wall. "So what's he waiting for now?"

Barone looked to Salvatore.

"He's waiting for you to blink. To soften. Because you have something he never had."

Salvatore stared at the map of his empire.

"He's waiting for a weakness."

Barone nodded. "And family makes men weak."

Salvatore turned slowly.

"No," he said. "Family makes men *careful*."

He pointed to a dot in southern Brooklyn. "We start here. The ports. If he's going to strike, he'll need an entry. I want every name that moves through that terminal watched."

Rico nodded. "We'll sweep the entire block. Quiet."

Claudia looked to Barone. "And if he doesn't come through the port?"

Barone smiled, slow and cold.

"Then he's already inside."

Frankie walked the edge of the frozen waterline that night, coat pulled tight, eyes scanning for movement.

He didn't like ghosts. Didn't trust legends. Barone was a story with a spine, and Ferri was a name spoken like a curse in the southern towns.

He paused near a container that shouldn't have been there. Markings scraped off. Padlock loose.

Inside: empty crates. A single envelope taped to the wall.

Frankie tore it down and opened it.

Inside, one photo.

A photo of Salvatore holding Joseph outside Eden.

And three words scrawled in black ink:

Blood births blood.

Back at the flat on Sullivan Street, Frankie slammed the photo down on the kitchen table.

Salvatore stared at it.

Rosa stood in the doorway, pale.

"Ferri's not coming," Salvatore said. "He's *here*."

Claudia entered with her gun half-drawn. "We've already got men sweeping the blocks. I'll triple the security."

Salvatore looked at the image again, then slowly slid it into the fireplace.

"He doesn't get in my house," he said. "He doesn't get near my son."

Rico loaded fresh bullets into his pistol. "Then we hunt him."

Salvatore nodded once.

"This war ends. Mine. My father's. Sicily's."

He looked to Rosa.

"For Joseph."

Part III - Three Nights Later - Carroll Street, Brooklyn

It started with fire.

A corner bakery, one of the fronts Salvatore had used to clean money for nearly a decade, was reduced to ash before sunrise. The blaze didn't spread, but the message did.

That same night, two of his longtime bookmen disappeared. One was found in a dumpster with his tongue cut out. The other never turned up at all.

By dawn, Luther Clay had confirmed three more crew members missing. All low-ranking. All part of the crew stationed near the Bronx.

Claudia read the names like they were already headstones.

"Mancini," she said. "Has to be."

Salvatore stood silently at the head of the table in Eden's backroom, his eyes fixed on the window, watching snow melt into grime.

Rico slammed his fist on the table. "This is it. This is his line in the sand."

"No," Salvatore said. "This is his *desperation*."

He turned.

"Carlo waited too long. Now he's overreaching."

Frankie lit a cigarette, voice low. "If he's swinging, he's hoping to draw blood fast. We hit back, it's full war."

"He already started one," Claudia muttered. "We just didn't announce it."

Salvatore nodded.

"Then it's time we do."

Carlo sat by the fire in his estate, blanket across his lap. His hands trembled slightly as he adjusted his cufflinks, but his eyes still burned with clarity.

Luca Greco entered with a smirk. "We made noise."

Carlo looked up. "Noise doesn't win wars."

"We hit three fronts. Pulled five of his earners off the street. The bakery's ashes are still warm. He hasn't responded."

Carlo stood slowly, ignoring the ache in his legs.

"He will. And when he does, it won't be with bullets."

He approached the window.

"He'll start peeling off captains. Making deals. That's his way."

Luca raised an eyebrow. "Then what do we do?"

Carlo's voice dropped.

"We remind him that before he built anything, we *owned* this city."

It was midnight. Joseph was sleeping. The house was quiet.

Rosa stood in the kitchen, boiling water for tea, when she noticed the envelope slipped under the back door. The edges were dry. No footprints. No sound.

She picked it up and froze.

No address.

Just one word on the front:

VITALI.

She didn't open it.

She called Salvatore.

He arrived within ten minutes, still buttoning his coat, eyes like stone.

Claudia, already behind him, swept the room, then took the envelope from Rosa.

She opened it with a blade.

Inside, a single item.

A note;

I watched him breathe.

Rosa sank into a chair, silent.

Salvatore took the photo and stared at it for a long time.

"Ferri," he said.

Claudia nodded.

Rico entered a moment later. "Mancini just hit another dock. Took out our Jersey runner."

"Two fronts," Claudia said. "They're testing your reach."

"No," Salvatore said. "They're trying to break my focus."

He looked to Rosa.

"They won't."

The crew assembled in full strength for the first time in weeks at the Red Hook warehouse. Armed, alert, and silent.

Salvatore entered through the back and climbed the stairs above the floor, looking down at the faces that made up his empire.

"These are the days where the city holds its breath," he said. "They wait to see which name fades next. Which street changes colors. Which blood flows fastest."

He walked the length of the catwalk.

"Carlo Mancini sent a message in fire. Adriano Ferri sent a whisper in red ink. I've heard both."

He paused, looking down.

"And now they'll hear mine."

Rico stepped forward. "How loud we talking?"

Salvatore looked him dead in the eye.

"Earthquake."

Adriano Ferri stood alone in a hotel suite that had once belonged to a Wall Street banker, staring at a corkboard full of faces and names.

At the center: Salvatore Vitali.

Beside it: Rosa. Joseph. Rico. Claudia. Eden.

He placed a fresh photo at the edge of the board.

The bakery—burned out, gutted.

He smiled faintly.

"They're all too busy watching the flames," he whispered in Sicilian. "They never see the match."

He reached into a drawer, pulled out a locket, and held it in his palm.

Inside: a photo of a man buried in Palermo soil.

His father.

Claudia joined Salvatore beneath the stars.

She handed him a folder. "Luca Greco is vulnerable. He's cut corners, skimmed off Mancini's books. We flip him, we get half of Carlo's reach overnight."

Salvatore nodded. "Do it."

She lit a cigarette. "And Ferri?"

"He wants fear," Salvatore said. "So we give him silence."

"Silence?" she asked.

"Yes," he said. "The kind that comes before the storm."

He looked out across the city.

"I promised Rosa this war would be my last. And it will be."

He turned back to her.

"But first, we finish what Carlo started."

15

Aldo's Betrayal

Part I - Early Spring, 1926 – Eden, The Garden

There were some faces you trusted because you'd grown up with them. Others, because they'd bled beside you. And some rare ones, you trusted because they had no reason to betray you.

Aldo Rossi had been all three.

Salvatore had known him since the earliest days in Brooklyn, when the names were whispered and the streets were dirt. Aldo had been there before the first crate of Cuban rum, before the first bribe, before Eden opened its doors. When Aldo smiled, it was with crooked teeth and half a promise—but it always felt honest.

So when Claudia placed the file on Salvatore's desk that morning, she didn't say a word.

She didn't need to.

Salvatore read the first page. Then the second. Then the ledger entries. The wiretap transcript. The note passed to one of Carlo Mancini's couriers two nights ago.

The name signed at the bottom.

A. Rossi.

Salvatore set the paper down slowly, as though it weighed more than he could lift.

Claudia finally spoke. "We triple-checked. Rico's guy heard it straight from one of Mancini's own mouthpieces. Aldo gave them routes. Schedules. Payment drops."

"Which ones?"

"Brooklyn North. Three runners. One shell company. The numbers laundering through Jersey."

He was quiet.

"And he did it for free," Claudia added. "Not money. Not leverage. He said it was a *favor*."

That word hung in the air like smoke.

Rico stared at the file later that afternoon, shaking his head.

"No. Not Aldo."

"It's real," Claudia said. "We followed the paper. He gave them *our veins*, Rico."

Frankie punched a wall. "He's family."

"No," Salvatore said quietly. "He was."

Frankie turned. "You want me to handle it?"

"No."

Rico cracked his knuckles. "Let me talk to him first. Maybe it's a misunderstanding."

Claudia rolled her eyes. "They don't *misunderstand* which families they sell us to."

But Salvatore raised a hand.

"No. I'll do it."

He met him at the Old Dockside Bar in Bay Ridge. The place hadn't changed in a decade. Same scratched oak bar, same cloudy mirror, same bartender who remembered every name and forgot every confession.

Aldo Rossi sat in the booth by the back window, sipping his whiskey like a man who didn't know the city was already whispering about him.

Salvatore entered alone.

He didn't sit. He didn't smile.

Aldo looked up. "Sal."

No answer.

Aldo's smile faltered. "You hear about the bakery?"

"I heard."

"Tough break."

Silence.

Aldo shifted. "You here for something, or—?"

Salvatore pulled the folded paper from his coat and dropped it on the table.

Aldo didn't touch it.

"Go ahead," Salvatore said.

Aldo sighed. "You had to know eventually."

Salvatore's eyes hardened. "Know what?"

"That this thing you built? It doesn't have a soul anymore."

Salvatore didn't move. "You gave our bloodline to Mancini."

"I gave *balance* to the city. You're choking it, Sal. You and your vision, your rules, your silence. Carlo—he may be old, but he understands what the city needs."

"What it *needs*?" Salvatore echoed.

Aldo leaned forward. "It needs order. And you forgot that."

Salvatore's voice dropped to a whisper. "You think order built Eden?"

"I think order kept it *alive.*"

A long pause.

"You're dead," Salvatore said, softly.

Aldo blinked.

"You've been dead since you handed them those names."

"Come on, Sal—"

"You'll leave New York tonight. You won't take a phone call. You won't send a letter. You'll never use the name Rossi again."

Aldo stood slowly. "Or what?"

Salvatore didn't blink.

"Or I bury your bones in a box without a label."

Rosa sat on the sofa with Joseph asleep in her arms later that night.

Salvatore poured himself a drink, his hands shaking just enough to spill a few drops on the counter.

"He was family," she said.

"He *was.*"

"And now?"

Salvatore drained the glass in one motion.

"Now he's a ghost."

By sunrise, the city had whispered fast.

By morning, Aldo Rossi was gone.

He left his apartment key with his sister. He left no note. No money. No phone calls.

But taped to the door of a small florist off Columbia Street— a place Salvatore's mother used to buy lilacs from—was a single sheet of paper.

A message.

Written in block letters.

FEAR NEVER DIES.
Rico read it first.
Then he burned it.

Claudia finished sweeping the upper floors of the Eden when she found the second envelope—this one slipped under the ledgers in Salvatore's private study.

Another note. And a name scrawled in black marker.
ADRIANO.
Salvatore stared at it for a long time before speaking.
"Two fronts," he murmured.
"We're stretched," Claudia warned.
"No," Salvatore said, voice like a blade.
"We're focused."

Part II - Same Day – Midtown, Mancini Social Club

Luca Greco leaned over the pool table in the backroom, cue chalked and untouched. The record player played faint jazz from a wall speaker, but no one listened. Four of his men waited behind him, silent. Waiting for orders.

Carlo Mancini entered with a cane in hand, flanked by two guards in gray wool coats. He took a seat slowly, his breath short, his patience shorter.

"Well?" Carlo asked.
Luca turned, face blank.
"Vitali's hurting."
Carlo raised a brow. "Just hurting?"
"He just cut Aldo Rossi loose. Ordered him out of the city."

"Alive?"

"For now."

Carlo shook his head in disappointment. "A mistake."

"No," Luca said. "It shows restraint. But it also shows he's still tied to the past. You'd have buried Aldo."

"I *will*," Carlo muttered. "When the time comes."

Luca walked over to the table, placed a folder in front of his boss.

"Next phase," he said. "We push into Red Hook. Quiet, not loud. No soldiers. Businessmen. Permits. Fronts."

Carlo opened the folder. It was all there—real estate deeds, shell LLCs, rezoning applications.

"If we walk in before he can close the door," Luca continued, "we plant our flag *inside* the empire."

Carlo smiled.

"Do it."

Salvatore stared down at the Eden blackboard covered in names and numbers. The city had been broken into colored zones. Most were white—safe. A few were red—compromised. And now, two more were orange.

Contested.

He circled them with chalk.

Claudia watched from the doorway. "Greco's expanding. We're hearing word of fronts opening under false LLCs. Dockside offices, warehouse leases, even a bakery."

"They want to bleed us from inside," Salvatore said. "Easier than shooting in the street."

Frankie lit a cigarette. "So we shut 'em down?"

"No," Salvatore said. "We buy them."

"What?"

"We buy the businesses they're using before they finish laundering the ownership."

He turned to Luther. "Get me a judge. One who owes us."

Luther nodded. "You want a freeze?"

"I want them frozen mid-move. Let Greco explain to Carlo how their silent takeover got caught in paperwork."

Claudia added, "It'll stall them. Not stop them."

"Long enough," Salvatore said, "for me to find the next traitor."

The bakery on Carroll Street looked like it had been there for twenty years. In truth, it had only opened two weeks ago. The ovens hadn't even been turned on.

It was a shell.

Salvatore arrived in the back of a delivery van with Rico and two soldiers. They slipped in through the alley, bypassing the fake security, and entered through the kitchen.

Inside, no pastries. No flour. Just folding chairs, crates labeled as "imported saffron," and three quiet men in suits who didn't recognize Salvatore until he spoke.

"This is my city," he said.

They froze.

Rico drew his pistol.

"No," Salvatore said. "Tell your boss to pack this place by tomorrow."

The tallest man—a Russian with a Bronx accent—spoke. "This is Luca Greco's property."

"Wrong," Salvatore replied. "This is a Vitali block. And Luca doesn't have the stomach to hold turf without someone else lighting the torch."

He handed the man a note.

"One day. Then fire."

They left without another word.

Claudia parked at the edge of the river by the Brooklyn Bridge and waited.

The message had gone out at midnight. A small-time informant on Greco's payroll wanted to talk. Offered a location. Promised truth.

She wasn't expecting a ghost.

The man who approached was thin, hollow-eyed, lips twitching from nicotine withdrawal. He handed her a manila envelope without speaking. She opened it.

Blueprints. Lease transfers. Dock schedules.

And at the bottom—a name.

Emilio Cerone.

Claudia frowned. "He's dead."

The man shook his head. "No. He's running Greco's shadow routes. Quiet. Under another name. He's the one laundering Mancini's cash through Tampa now."

She snapped the folder shut.

"You just earned yourself a favor."

The man nodded and disappeared into the mist.

Salvatore stood over Joseph's crib for a long moment. The boy slept soundly, fists tucked under his chin.

Rosa watched from the doorway.

"You're slipping away again," she said.

He looked up, eyes hollow. "No."

"You're going deeper into this."

"I have to."

Rosa walked over, wrapped her arms around him.

"You told me this would be the last war."

"It will be."

She pressed her forehead to his chest. "Then win it. Quickly."

At the Federal Courthouse, Luther stood beside Judge Harmon as the clerk filed the emergency motion.

Twelve Mancini shell companies.

Eight connected LLCs.

Three storefronts.

All frozen pending an investigation into financial irregularities.

No blood spilled.

But a message sent.

By noon, the news reached Luca Greco.

He didn't throw the folder.

He burned it.

Later that night, on the Eden roof, Claudia handed Salvatore the envelope from the river.

He read it silently.

"Cerone," he said. "I should've known."

"You want him found?"

"No," Salvatore said. "I want him *isolated*. Then squeezed."

He looked out over the skyline.

"Greco thinks he's clever. Mancini thinks he's inevitable."

Claudia tilted her head. "And you?"

"I'm patient."

He turned to her.

"Let them keep planting flags."

He crushed his cigarette underfoot.

"I'm laying traps."

Part III - 48 Hours Later - Tampa Front, Port Authority Office

The rain came down in heavy sheets, soaking the dockhands and muting the crackle of radios. Inside the port authority's central office, Emilio Cerone shuffled papers, checking falsified manifests and coded invoices.

He didn't see the two men enter behind him.

The first placed a gloved hand on his shoulder. The second locked the door.

By the time Cerone turned around, it was too late.

No questions were asked.

No warnings given.

Just a ledger removed, a briefcase taken, and a body left on the floor, slumped over the desk.

When the morning shift arrived, the documents had vanished—and with them, Greco's southern laundering channel.

Back in New York, Salvatore received a single call.

Rico's voice was cold: "It's done."

Claudia stood in the kitchen, thumbing through the port transfer documents they'd pulled from Cerone's desk.

"Greco won't recover this fast," she said. "It's a central artery. You just cut off his funding."

Salvatore nodded slowly. "Now we wait to see how he bleeds."

Frankie poured coffee. "He won't go quiet."

"No," Salvatore said. "But he'll go *loud*. And that's when we'll catch him overreaching."

He looked at Claudia.

"Put eyes on his family fronts. I want to see what he sacrifices to stay loyal to Carlo."

Claudia raised an eyebrow. "You think he'll burn his own?"

"No," Salvatore said. "But he'll bleed them if he has to."

Luca Greco stood before Carlo Mancini at the Social Club, face like stone, jaw clenched.

"He got Cerone," Luca said. "Our entire Tampa line is dust."

Carlo exhaled through his nose. "And what did I tell you?"

Luca's voice was low. "That Salvatore doesn't fight wars. He fights *systems*."

Carlo leaned forward. "Then break his. Don't shoot his soldiers. Don't torch his bars. Shake his *foundation*."

Luca nodded. "Understood."

Carlo's tone hardened. "No mistakes, Luca."

"I don't make them."

The black car pulled up in front of an elementary school in Brooklyn Heights as dusk fell.

The driver waited exactly three minutes before stepping out and slipping a manila envelope into the mailbox labeled: St. Clement's Parish Office.

Inside: photos of Rosa and Joseph.

Walking. Shopping. Laughing.

Daily routines.

Every one timestamped.

And beneath them, in red ink, scrawled in delicate, foreign

handwriting:

Soon.

The envelope was delivered to Eden by midnight.

Claudia opened it.

She said nothing.

Just handed it to Salvatore.

He stared at the images, jaw locked.

Frankie swore under his breath. "That's Greco."

"Or someone working for him," Claudia said.

Salvatore's eyes narrowed.

"No," he said quietly. "This isn't Greco. This is Ferri."

He folded the photos and tucked them into his coat.

Then turned to the room.

"Bring in the Florentine broker," he said.

Claudia blinked. "You mean the guy who handles property sweeps for overseas outfits?"

"Yes," Salvatore said. "We're not taking territory anymore. We're *acquiring* it."

Three Bensonhurts businesses owned by Greco's cousin were bought within eight hours that next day.

A butcher shop. A wine bar. A transport garage.

The broker used a Swiss holding firm with a different name on every lease.

By the time Greco heard about it, his cousin had already called him in tears, evicted, bankrupt, and owed nothing.

Greco put a bullet through his office window.

Rosa found Salvatore watching the city burn orange beneath the falling sun. She didn't speak right away.

When she did, her voice was quiet.

"Did you see the photos?"

He nodded.

"They know our route to the market. They know when I drop Joseph off at church. They know—"

"I know," Salvatore said.

"And what are you doing about it?"

He turned to her.

"I'm building a city they can't walk through without asking *me* for the right to breathe."

Rosa shook her head. "Joseph doesn't need a throne, Sal. He needs a *father*."

"I can be both."

"Not for long."

She left before he could answer.

Carlo sipped his tea with hands that no longer shook. Across from him, Luca Greco paced.

"He's carving me piece by piece," Luca said. "And every time I hit back, he hits lower."

"Good," Carlo said.

Greco stopped. "Good?"

"You're bleeding," Carlo replied. "That means you're close to the vein."

Carlo looked up, eyes shining.

"We've pushed him into protecting his family. That means he's off balance. Now we press."

Greco nodded slowly. "What if he pushes back harder?"
Carlo smiled faintly.
"Then we take the gloves off."

16

The Waterfront Pact

Part I - One Week Later - Lower Manhattan, Old Customs House

Rain streaked the grand windows of the old customs house, a building that had seen deals struck and empires rise behind its marbled halls long before any of the Five Families had names carved in blood.

Salvatore Vitali stood at the center of the great hall, alone but not unarmed. Rico flanked the rear exit. Frankie waited on the roof. Claudia had chosen the venue for its strategic control: one entrance, one exit, no blindsides.

Salvatore adjusted his cuffs and checked the time.

Marco Lombardi was late.

That wasn't unusual.

Lombardi had a reputation for treating punctuality like weakness. He arrived when it suited him—and usually with a drink already in hand.

Today, however, he arrived quietly. No entourage. No

theater. Just the sound of a light thud of polished shoes.

He smiled like an old friend who'd once stabbed you and felt bad about it later.

"Salvatore," he said warmly. "You look taller since the last time we tried to kill each other."

Salvatore didn't smile. "I didn't invite you for nostalgia."

Marco eased himself onto a wooden bench and pulled out a silver case of cigarettes.

"No," he said. "You invited me because you're bleeding from two sides and want to make sure the third doesn't open up."

Salvatore didn't deny it. "I'm offering the Lombardi Family protection—quiet protection. Shipping routes, cold storage, some labor connections. In exchange, you keep DeMarco where he is."

Marco lit a cigarette, studying Salvatore through the smoke. "You always deal like a banker. Clean, quiet. But you're a butcher beneath the skin. That's why I like you."

"I don't care if you like me," Salvatore said. "I care if you'll hold DeMarco back."

Marco exhaled slowly. "Vincent's been hungry since Carlo Mancini started slipping. You've hurt Mancini, so now DeMarco thinks it's his turn."

"Then make him think twice," Salvatore said.

Marco leaned forward. "And why would I do that?"

Salvatore's voice dropped. "Because if he tips this war into chaos, the Feds won't knock on Mancini's door. Or mine. They'll knock on yours."

Marco's eyes narrowed. "You'd go that far?"

"No," Salvatore said. "*DeMarco* would. And when he does, the headlines won't say 'DeMarco Family Raided.' They'll say 'Lombardi Scandal Exposes New York Underworld.'"

Marco studied him in silence.

Then, finally: "You've gotten sharper."

"I've had to."

A pause.

Marco flicked ash to the floor.

"You give me the docks south of Flatbush, and I'll keep DeMarco leashed."

Salvatore didn't blink. "Done."

Marco smiled. "You're learning how this game is played, Salvatore."

"I'm not playing," he said. "I'm ending it."

Rico laid out a map on the long oak table in the Eden back room, red pins in the south, black in the north, and one golden tack marking the DeMarco safe zone.

"Lombardi wants Flatbush," Rico said. "That's real estate we could've held."

"We can't hold it *and* hold the city," Salvatore replied. "Lombardi's leash on DeMarco is worth more than the property."

Frankie grunted. "So we're giving ground now?"

"No," Claudia said, entering with a fresh report. "We're *purchasing leverage.*"

She handed the report to Salvatore.

"Two DeMarco enforcers moved toward Williamsburg yesterday. They turned around once they saw Vitali men on the block. Word travels fast."

Rico nodded. "So it's working."

Salvatore looked over the room.

"For now. But DeMarco's ambition is like a fever. It might break—or boil over."

Vincent DeMarco swirled his brandy and stared at the letter Marco Lombardi had sent him that morning.

Pull back, or I pull rank.

Vincent's lip curled. "He thinks he owns me."

His consigliere, Matteo, poured himself a drink. "He does. Technically. He has more manpower."

Vincent stood. "Not for long."

Matteo raised an eyebrow. "What are you thinking?"

Vincent walked to the window and stared out into the night.

"I'm thinking I find out how deep Vitali's roots go. If I can't move forward, maybe I tunnel under."

Salvatore stood by Joseph's crib again.

The boy reached for his finger, small and trusting.

Rosa leaned against the doorway.

"You keep giving away pieces of this city. How much will be left?"

Salvatore looked up at her.

"Enough for him."

She stepped forward, wrapped her arms around him.

"Then make sure that's true."

He nodded once.

"I will."

Part II - Three Days Later - Williamsburg, Brooklyn

The butcher shop had two front windows, each fogged by the morning chill, and a tin bell that rang once when Claudia stepped inside. The air smelled of copper and salt, fresh sausage hanging in loops behind the counter.

She waited until the counterman, a gaunt man with cloudy eyes and a missing thumb, finished wrapping a package for the housewife ahead of her. Then he glanced her way, nodded once, and disappeared through a curtain behind the hanging meats.

A moment later, a younger man emerged from the back—a wiry kid in his twenties named Lino Ferrera, with dark curls and a twitchy demeanor.

"You're the one Lombardi sent?" he asked in a thick Bronx accent.

"I'm the one *Vitali* sent," Claudia corrected.

He smirked, chewing on a toothpick. "Same thing now, ain't it?"

"No," she said. "It's not."

He led her through the backroom—past the cutting station and walk-in freezer—to a cellar door that opened into a cramped space beneath the butcher shop. Inside were two other men, both mid-level soldiers in DeMarco's outer circle, both recently flipped.

A single lantern illuminated the room.

Claudia crossed her arms. "What do you have?"

Lino handed over a folder, bound with twine. Inside: names, drop sites, and surveillance logs—pictures sketched, not taken. No cameras. Just sharp pencils and steady hands.

"They're watching your movements," Lino said. "Not just yours. Rico, Luther, that mouthy guy—Frankie."

Claudia flipped through the pages, each one confirming what she suspected.

"DeMarco doesn't trust Lombardi," she said.

"He doesn't trust *anyone*," Lino replied. "He's building a side alliance. Something quiet. Small crews. Not DeMarco colors, not Five Families. Outsiders. Some guys from Philly. Even talk of Sicilian mercs."

Claudia stopped flipping. "Mercs?"

"Off-the-boat types. Quiet, clean, and expensive. He's funneling cash through an art dealer in SoHo to pay them."

Claudia tied the folder shut.

"Keep watching. Any names, I want them yesterday."

She paused at the cellar door.

"And if you're lying to me, Lino—"

"I know," he said, backing away slightly. "Vitali doesn't forget."

She didn't answer.

She didn't need to.

Claudia slammed the folder down on the Eden back room table.

"He's digging a tunnel," she said. "Under both us and Lombardi."

Salvatore opened the file, scanning the contents quickly, his expression unreadable.

Rico frowned. "Philly crews?"

"Some," Claudia said. "And something else. Sicilians. Not Ferri's men—new ones."

Frankie leaned against the wall. "DeMarco's trying to build an army off the books."

"He wants plausible deniability," Claudia said. "If it fails, he blames outsiders. If it works, he controls the fallout."

Salvatore closed the folder. "Then we break the dealer."

"What dealer?" Frankie asked.

Claudia answered. "Art dealer in SoHo. Named Enrico

Damasso. He's a middleman. Probably doesn't even know who he's feeding money to."

"Then he's a loose thread," Salvatore said. "And I want him pulled."

Rico nodded. "We'll bring him in."

Salvatore raised a hand. "No. Not yet. We let him run. See where his leash goes."

The Damasso Gallery was white walls and soft jazz, overpriced absinthe behind a lacquered counter, and paintings no one could afford unless they were hiding something.

Enrico Damasso smiled too easily and sweated too quickly for a man who claimed to deal in Monet and Modigliani.

He didn't see the man tailing him.

Didn't see the car parked two blocks over with Luther Clay inside, watching with opera glasses through a newspaper.

Didn't see the note passed to a courier in a gray coat at precisely 2:14 p.m.

But Claudia did.

She watched from the café across the street, fingers wrapped around a cup of tea gone cold, eyes never leaving the gallery.

By the time the courier disappeared into the alley behind the gallery, Claudia was already up and moving.

Rosa placed a record on the player and let the scratchy piano notes fill the air. Salvatore sat nearby, coat still on, mind clearly elsewhere.

She poured him a drink and handed it over.

"Lombardi holding?"

"For now."

"DeMarco?"

"Clawing in the dark."

Rosa leaned against the wall. "And Ferri?"

Salvatore stared into the amber liquid in his glass.

"Soon," he said.

Rosa's voice dropped. "Do you think they're connected?"

"I think DeMarco's too proud to know he's being used."

"And Ferri?"

"He's too smart to strike before he's sure we're blind."

Vincent DeMarco sat beneath a red lamp, the glow casting strange shadows across his features. Matteo poured him a fresh drink and dropped a sealed envelope on the table.

"What's this?" Vincent asked.

"Report from Damasso. The courier delivered. But there was a tail."

Vincent's smile vanished.

"A tail?"

"Woman. Brunette. Quick."

Vincent's expression soured.

"Claudia."

He stood.

"Time to smoke her out."

Matteo raised an eyebrow. "You want to go loud?"

"No," Vincent said. "I want to go *invisible*. I want to bleed Vitali where he doesn't see it coming."

He tapped the envelope once.

"Tell the Sicilians. Move up the timeline."

Claudia stood beside Salvatore as wind swept off the East River. She handed him a list—names and wire routes, all tied to DeMarco's quiet push.

"They're getting bolder," she said.

"And more desperate," Salvatore added.

She lit a cigarette. "Lombardi still in?"

"For now," Salvatore said. "But if DeMarco moves too fast, he'll break the leash."

Claudia looked out over the city.

"What then?"

Salvatore didn't answer.

He didn't need to.

The wind did it for him—cold, rising, and coming from every direction.

Part III - Late Evening - Long Island Estate, Private Garden Room

The room smelled of old wood and imported Sicilian lemon trees. Outside, the waves hit the rocks with rhythm, distant and unfelt.

Vincent DeMarco sat across from Adriano Ferri, the man whose silence was heavier than gunfire. His face was unmarked, his clothes immaculate, but his eyes—black and still—were what made Vincent uncomfortable.

It was said Ferri never spoke first.

Tonight was no exception.

"I've kept my leash tight," Vincent began. "I've held back while the city turns. While Carlo fades and Lombardi plays both sides."

Ferri blinked once.

"But I'm losing ground. Every day, Vitali takes more without firing a bullet. And now? Now his woman's watching me. His soldiers are in my shadows. And Lombardi won't lift a finger unless someone else breaks the peace."

He leaned forward.

"You want blood. I want control. So I'm saying it plainly."

He slid a folder across the table.

"Finish this. Take the boy. Take the woman. Put a knife through Salvatore's legacy. And I'll make sure the door stays open when it's done."

Ferri opened the folder.

Inside: photos of Rosa, Joseph, the Sullivan Street flat.

He didn't speak.

Just smiled.

Then folded the file neatly, stood, and left the room without a word.

DeMarco exhaled and looked to Matteo.

"It's started."

The fire crackled as Carlo Mancini stirred his tea. Across from him, Luca Greco reviewed a street map of downtown Brooklyn and Queens.

"We hit two fronts," Luca said. "One symbolic, one strategic."

He pointed.

"Symbolic: Eden. We blow the foundation of his pride to hell. Strategic: the cold storage near the ferry docks. That cripples his distribution."

Carlo nodded slowly. "And we make it loud."

"Loud enough to remind the city who built the streets Salvatore's trying to pave."

Carlo looked up. "And the family?"

"We send warnings. Empty graves. Unmarked letters. Let

fear do the bleeding first."

Carlo raised his cup. "Then do it."

Luca folded the map. "It's already in motion."

Salvatore couldn't sleep that night.

He stood by the window, cigarette burning down to the filter, watching the alley like it might speak to him.

Claudia entered quietly. "We've tracked DeMarco's courier back to a secondary residence. Unmarked. Not under his name."

Salvatore didn't look away. "Ferri?"

"No sign. But DeMarco's cutting corners. Fast money. Faster alliances. Desperate."

Salvatore turned to her. "What would you do?"

"Expose him."

"No," he said. "Not yet. He wants fire. Let's see what burns."

He crushed the cigarette out.

Then, softly: "Double the guards on Rosa and Joseph."

Adriano Ferri stood alone on the Brooklyn Bridge, watching as the ships cut through the waves toward the city's edge.

In his coat pocket, he carried a blade that had slit three throats in Palermo before the war.

In his mind, he carried only one name.

Vitali.

He whispered it once, just above the roar of the wind.

And the storm began to rise.

17

Ashes and Vows

Part I - Predawn - Sullivan Street Flat

Rosa woke to silence.

It wasn't the peaceful quiet of sleep, but the kind that made the hairs on the back of her neck rise. Joseph stirred beside her in the bassinet, fingers twitching in a dream. A faint creak from downstairs snapped her fully awake.

She rose without sound, bare feet on the cold floor, reaching instinctively for the revolver Salvatore had hidden in the drawer beside the crib.

Another creak. Slower this time.

She held her breath.

The doorknob turned.

Before she could aim, a figure moved fast through the shadows, knocking her hand away, pinning her to the wall.

"You don't know me," the man said in Italian-accented English, "but I've known your husband my whole life."

His face was calm. Still. Like death had already decided.

Adriano Ferri.

He held a blade—old, worn, black-handled. His other hand reached toward Joseph.

"No!" Rosa screamed, twisting violently and shoving her elbow into Ferri's ribs. He grunted and staggered back, not expecting resistance. She grabbed the drawer again, this time getting the revolver.

She raised it, shaking.

A shot rang out. But not from her gun.

Ferri vanished into the hallway as a second figure charged in.

Barone.

Smoke trailed from his revolver. "Go!" he shouted to Rosa. "Take the boy!"

Rosa scooped Joseph from the crib and ducked behind the bed.

Barone moved cautiously into the hallway, gun leading his step.

"Come out, Adriano!" Barone shouted. "You came across the sea to die?"

"You should've died in Sicily," Ferri hissed from the shadows.

Another shot. The bullet slammed into the wall inches from Barone's head. He dove sideways into the guest room. Ferri darted past the door, fast as a shadow.

The creak of the floor gave him away. Barone fired again— missed. Ferri lunged, blade flashing. They struggled in the hallway, crashing into the wallpaper, knocking over a framed photo of Salvatore's parents.

Barone got a hand on Ferri's wrist, trying to stop the knife. Ferri slammed his forehead into Barone's nose.

Blood burst. Barone dropped his weapon.

The knife plunged forward.

Barone caught it with both hands, struggling. "You're a coward," he spat.

"And you're an old man," Ferri growled.

The knife sank deep into Barone's chest.

He gasped—once, twice—and went still.

Ferri yanked the blade free and turned.

He took three steps back toward the bedroom. He locked eyes with Rosa and a wicked grin creeped on his face.

But Salvatore had returned.

No warning. Just fury.

The first shot caught Ferri in the leg from behind, spinning him sideways.

The second hit his shoulder, blowing blood across the hallway.

Ferri dropped to one knee. Raised his blade. Spat blood.

"You were always a child in a man's world, Vitali," he hissed.

The third shot silenced him.

Square to the chest.

Ferri slumped forward, knife still in his hand.

Salvatore walked up to him, stepped on the blade, and leaned down.

"This is for Rosa."

He fired once more into Ferri's skull.

The silence afterward was worse than the noise.

He rushed back to the bedroom.

Rosa sat on the floor, Joseph cradled in her arms, tears running silently down her cheeks.

Salvatore sank to his knees beside them.

"I thought I could control this," he whispered.

"You never could," she said. "Not all of it."

He kissed Joseph's forehead.

"Then it ends. Tonight."

Claudia swept the back room of the Eden with her sidearm still drawn. Frankie locked the doors. Rico stood at the bar, reloading.

"We got hit," Claudia said, flatly.

"Ferri?" Frankie asked.

"Dead," Salvatore answered, voice hollow. "But not before Barone took the blade."

Rico muttered a prayer under his breath. "He was the last tie to the old country."

Salvatore nodded. "And now he's the last man who ever saw my father alive."

He looked around the room.

"Double security. Pull in everyone. Mancini and DeMarco will hear about this by sunrise. And when they do, they'll think we're weak."

Claudia's eyes narrowed. "Then let's remind them what we are."

Part II - Same Day - Midmorning - Eden, The Garden

The snow outside had begun to melt into sludge, but inside Eden, the air was cold with tension. Salvatore hadn't slept. He stood at the window overlooking the alley where a body had once been dumped in the early days, back when Eden had been more ambition than power.

Claudia laid the morning report on the table without a word.

Frankie leaned against the far wall, bruises still blooming from the night before.

"They're moving," Claudia said. "Fast."

"Who?" Salvatore asked, though he already knew.

"Mancini. Greco's behind the logistics, but this has Carlo's hands all over it."

Rico entered, a bloodstained bandage on his shoulder.

"They hit me in daylight. Two of them, posing as cops. Took a shot at the car. Glass exploded—got me in the shoulder."

Salvatore nodded. "And?"

"They're dead."

"Good."

Claudia continued, "It wasn't just Rico. They tried to grab Luther last night. Black car tailed him from his club to the bridge. He got away, but barely. Shot out one of their tires, ducked through the Navy Yard."

"Anyone else?"

"Frankie."

Frankie gave a bitter laugh. "Tried to burn down my aunt's grocery. She wasn't even in it. Just the building. Set a Molotov through the side window and ran. Kids saw them and screamed. That's what saved the place."

Salvatore turned away from the window.

"They're trying to shake us. Cut the roots."

Frankie pushed off the wall. "So what's the play?"

"Let them think they're winning," Salvatore said. "We hold position. We tighten the circle. We make them feel like they've got us by the throat."

He paused.

"Then we remind them—"

"We're the ones with the blade," Claudia finished.

Luca Greco lit a cigar slowly, savoring the crackle of the leaf before taking the first drag at the Mancini Social Club.

"They're still breathing," he said.

Carlo Mancini sipped his coffee. "Then we breathe harder."

Luca smiled. "We gave them blood. Fear. Noise. And they stayed quiet."

"They're waiting," Carlo said. "Salvatore is cautious. It's his strength and his weakness."

"We keep pressing?"

"No," Carlo said. "Not yet."

Luca frowned.

Carlo leaned forward. "Now we sow *doubt*. In the city. In their allies. We let the streets start asking—'Can the Vitalis really protect anyone?'"

"And when they start whispering?"

"We start carving."

Rosa fed Joseph slowly that evening, her hands shaking more than she'd admit. The room felt darker since the night before, even with the sun still fading behind the city's silhouette.

Salvatore entered, blood on his collar, soot on his coat. He knelt beside them.

"You're safe," he said.

"For now," Rosa replied.

He looked at Joseph, then to her. "You want me to stop."

She didn't answer.

"I can't," he said. "Not yet."

She nodded, lips tight.

"Just make sure that when it ends, we still have something to come back to."

He kissed Joseph's head.

"I promise."

Frankie cleaned his pistol by lamplight outside the East River Docks. Rico sat beside him, arm in a sling, sipping whiskey through a cracked glass.

"They came close," Rico muttered.

Frankie didn't look up. "Not close enough."

"You think Carlo's coming next?"

Frankie finally looked at him. "Carlo doesn't get his hands dirty anymore."

"No," Claudia said, entering. "But he gives the orders. And I think the next one's going to bleed."

She dropped a map on the table—three red Xs, marked across Brooklyn and Queens.

"What are we looking at?" Frankie asked.

"Supply lines," Claudia said. "And pressure points. They're trying to box us in. Cut movement. Control perception."

Rico smirked. "Then we cut back."

Salvatore entered behind her, calm but cold.

"No," he said. "We don't *cut back*."

They turned to him.

"Now we *burn forward*."

A young man stepped inside the Church Street Cafe, carrying a letter folded twice and sealed with a plain wax stamp.

He handed it to the bartender and left without a word.

The bartender gave it to his cousin, a known Mancini affiliate.

Inside the letter: one sentence written in bold, block script.

You missed. We won't.

Part III - Midnight - South Williamsburg, "The Crimson Room" Speakeasy (Mancini-Owned)

The Crimson Room had once been the crown jewel of Carlo Mancini's public face—a place where politicians, entertainers, and racketeers rubbed shoulders beneath chandeliers and drank behind bulletproof doors.

Tonight, the doors were unlocked.

The floor was mostly empty—only a few loyalists playing cards in the back and a bartender polishing glasses with a knowing smirk. They were expecting a quiet night. Routine protection. Routine payoffs.

They did not expect the sound of the front doors opening without a knock.

They did not expect the figure who walked in—long coat, black gloves, eyes like winter.

Salvatore Vitali.

He didn't speak.

He didn't raise a gun.

He just walked slowly to the center of the room, placed a sealed envelope on the bar, and gave the bartender a quiet nod.

Then he turned around and left.

Five minutes later, the back exit burst open again—this time with two men in gas masks and overalls.

One carried a steel drum. The other, a fuse box.

The bartender's scream was never heard.

Across the street, Frankie lit a cigarette as flames curled up through the windows of The Crimson Room.

Claudia watched the fire take hold of the velvet curtains

and mahogany fixtures. Bottles exploded behind the bar like fireworks.

Rico exhaled slowly, his arm still wrapped in bandages.

Salvatore stood in silence, coat flicking in the wind, his jaw locked.

"She was Carlo's first," Claudia said. "That speakeasy helped bankroll half his judges in the 1900s."

Salvatore didn't blink.

"She was his pride," he said. "Now she's ashes."

Carlo Mancini held the still-warm envelope in his hands at his estate.

The contents were simple.

A photo of the burned-out Crimson Room.

And a matchbook from Eden.

Inside, a single line handwritten in ink:

We don't bow. We bury.

Carlo's hands trembled.

Luca Greco entered moments later.

"He did it," Luca said. "Flat-out."

Carlo's jaw tightened. "Good."

"Good?"

Carlo's eyes burned.

"Now we stop pretending."

The city glowed orange in the distance, though it wasn't just the fire anymore. Sirens wailed like mourning bells, and Salvatore watched from his rooftop throne in silence.

Claudia joined him.

"No way Mancini stays quiet after this," she said.

"He doesn't need to," Salvatore replied. "He's already

roaring."

She handed him a new list—targets, whispers, safehouses.

"And what do we do now?"

He took a deep breath, eyes never leaving the skyline.

"Now?" he said.

"Now we go to war."

18

A Crown Made of Smoke

Part I - Early Morning - Red Hook Dockyards

Fog rolled over the piers like ghosts summoned for one last ritual. Ships sat still, their chains clinking like iron teeth. Crates stacked high turned the dock into a warren of shadow and angles.

It was here, in the oldest corner of the Brooklyn waterfront, that the final move began.

Salvatore Vitali stepped from the black car in silence. Claudia exited after him, checking her weapon beneath her coat. Frankie and Rico were already in position, rifles tucked under their long coats, eyes sweeping every rooftop.

"Place is dead quiet," Rico muttered. "Too quiet."

"It's not quiet," Claudia replied. "It's *waiting*."

Salvatore said nothing. His face was unreadable. He had come not for revenge or blood—he'd had that. Tonight, he came to break the chain that had held him since the first handshake with Carlo Mancini.

They were no longer student and master.

They were rivals.

And only one would walk out standing tall.

Carlo arrived with less ceremony, carried inside a covered black car, flanked by Luca Greco and two of his dead-eyed enforcers. He walked slower now, aided by a cane more ornate than practical, but his gaze was as sharp as ever.

"They'll have high ground," Luca muttered. "Want me to flood the east lot?"

"No," Carlo said. "This isn't a slaughter. It's a statement."

He stepped onto the main pier, where a tarp-covered platform stood between two rusted anchors. The place was chosen by design—neutral, but bleeding with history. Once, these docks had smuggled weapons for every family in New York. Now, they would host the reckoning.

The mist parted as Salvatore and Carlo faced each other at last.

No guards stood beside them. No weapons were raised.

Only two men.

Two legacies.

Two kings.

Carlo looked thinner. Older. His eyes, however, had lost none of their fire.

"You've burned my empire to the roots," he said.

"And you bled mine," Salvatore replied.

"You broke the rules."

"There are no rules left."

Carlo stepped forward. "I gave you power. I gave you *purpose.*"

"You gave me chains," Salvatore said coldly. "You treated my rise as your possession."

"You were a child when I found you."

"And now I'm the man who makes you kneel."

A long silence followed.

Then Carlo laughed, soft and broken. "Is that what you want, Salvatore? For me to bow? In front of your crew, your city, your *ghosts*?"

Salvatore stepped forward.

"I want this war to end. I want your hand off my family's throat. And I want every one of your captains to know that the Vitali name stands on its own."

"And if I refuse?" Carlo asked.

Salvatore's voice lowered. "Then this dock becomes a graveyard."

Ten Minutes Later

It came suddenly, not from the men beside either don, but from the rooftops, the cranes, and the cargo towers. A third party.

Shots cracked through the morning fog. Rifles echoed across the water.

"DOWN!" Claudia yelled, tackling Salvatore.

Luca cursed, dragging Carlo behind a crate. "It's not Vitali's crew—it's outsiders!"

"The Sicilians," Carlo spat. "DeMarco's trash."

Chaos erupted. Frankie and Rico opened fire, cutting down two shooters on the scaffold. Claudia picked off one who had tried to flank left.

Blood slicked the dock. Workers screamed from hidden offices.

For a moment, it looked like no one would survive.

But then the smoke cleared.

And only Vitali and Mancini remained.

Back to back.

Enemies five minutes ago.

Now fighting side by side.

One Hour Later

Bodies littered the pier.

Fifteen dead.

Seven wounded.

None from Salvatore's inner circle.

Carlo leaned against a crate, breath labored, one leg bleeding.

"You're too much like me," he said. "That's why this ends here."

Salvatore nodded. "You stay in Westchester. You keep your judges. But you leave the streets to me."

Carlo winced. "And what do I get?"

"Your life."

A long beat.

Then: "Fine."

The silence between them wasn't peace.

It was survival.

Rosa joined Salvatore beneath the open sky. The city glowed below, smoke curling from chimneys and ruins alike.

"You did it," she said.

"No," he replied. "I survived it."

He turned to her.

"But now they see me."

"They always saw you."

He shook his head. "No. They saw a man walking someone else's path. Now they see the man who burned it down."

From below, Claudia called up.

"Word's spreading. Mancini's pulled his men back. The war's cooling."

Salvatore lit a cigarette.

"Good. Let them breathe."

He looked out over the lights of New York.

"But not too deep. The fire's not out. Not yet."

Part II - Two Days Later - Eden, The Garden

The silence inside Eden wasn't peace—it was recovery. Men moved slower. Claudia walked with a slight limp. Frankie had bandages wrapped around his ribs and one arm. The bar was patched with fresh wood where bullet holes had shattered the old grain. But despite the bruises and blood, Eden still stood.

So did Salvatore.

He sat at the long oak table in the backroom, the ledger open before him, eyes fixed on the names written in his own hand.

Claudia entered with the morning's updates. "Mancini's men are pulling back. The west side's clean. Their Queens operation is quiet. Luca Greco hasn't been seen since the docks."

"Which means he's hiding or bleeding," Salvatore said, flipping a page. "Either way, he's no longer our concern."

Frankie stepped in behind her. "You really think Carlo's done?"

"No," Salvatore said. "But he knows now—if he wants to play king, he'll bleed like a pawn."

He closed the ledger.

"Now we take what's ours."

Rico met Salvatore at the recently vacated Mancini warehouse off Flushing Avenue. It had once been a key distribution hub— beer, tobacco, counterfeit stamps, and untraceable bills. Now it was stripped bare, the only signs of Mancini's presence the blood-stained floor and the faint smell of cheap cigars.

"You sure you want this one?" Rico asked. "It's still hot. Cops sniffed around last week."

"I don't want it," Salvatore said. "I want everyone to *see* I took it."

He turned to Claudia. "Have our men set up shop here. Make it clean. Legit, on paper. Real supply. No shells."

She nodded. "You want a flag, not a ghost."

"Exactly."

Marco Lombardi watched the city shift from behind his black-tinted window, swirling a glass of limoncello.

"Salvatore wins one war," he said aloud, "and the city starts calling him Caesar."

His consigliere leaned in. "He's moving fast. Docks, liquor, even some of the old Mancini cops. They're flipping."

Marco smirked. "They always flip when they smell fresh blood."

"You want to counter?"

"No," Marco said. "Let him build. The higher he climbs, the easier he is to see. The easier to… reach."

Joseph was sleeping. Rosa sat by the window, the evening paper folded in her lap. The front page showed flames over the docks and one single, grainy photo of Salvatore—shoulders squared, face cold, eyes shadowed beneath his hat.

The caption read: *"NEW DON RISES IN WAKE OF BROOK-LYN BLOODBATH."*

Rosa didn't know whether to feel pride or dread.

Salvatore entered quietly.

"Did you read it?" she asked, not turning around.

"I lived it," he replied.

She stood. "You've got the city now."

"No," he said, approaching. "I've got a piece of it. And every inch of it wants to take that piece back."

She looked up at him. "Then stop measuring your worth in territory."

"I can't," he said, voice low. "Not yet."

She nodded slowly.

"Then promise me something."

"Anything."

"When it's done… when they stop coming for us… you'll come back to *us*."

He touched her cheek.

"I swear."

It was a midnight meeting at Saint Casimir's Crypt. Salvatore, Claudia, and Rico met with four captains—one from each outer borough. Three had been neutral during the war. One had been quietly loyal to Mancini but now arrived alone.

Salvatore stood at the head of the tomb, his voice echoing softly in the cold stone.

"There's no more war. Not today. Not tomorrow. Not unless someone starts one."

The men nodded.

"I don't ask for your loyalty. I ask for your word. Keep your streets clean. Keep your crews tight. And if someone moves against me, you let me know before they bury you too."

The captains murmured assent.

Then the one from Queens, a wiry man named Calderone, stepped forward. "Word is DeMarco's been making calls."

Salvatore's eyes narrowed. "To who?"

"Can't say. But they're not local. Different dialect. Southern."

Claudia caught the glance. "Sicilian?"

"Maybe."

Salvatore didn't react, but the spark was there.

He thanked them and dismissed the meeting.

As they left, Claudia asked, "You think it's Ferri's old friends?"

"No," Salvatore said. "I think it's something worse."

The city skyline stretched before him on the Eden roof, flickering in the wind like a lit fuse.

Claudia joined him.

"Half the city bows. The other half watches."

Salvatore nodded. "And the ones who smile… sharpen knives behind their backs."

"You sure you're ready for this?"

He looked out over the boroughs, smoke still rising from a

chimney that once belonged to Mancini.

"I didn't come this far to stay safe," he said. "I came this far to rule."

Claudia smiled faintly. "Then rule."

Salvatore took a deep breath.

"Peace is a candle in the wind."

He exhaled.

"Let's see how long it burns."

Part III - Early Morning - Flushing Avenue, Former Mancini Clubhouse

The old Mancini speakeasy had been boarded up since the docks burned. For decades, it had been the unofficial throne room of the Mancini family—back when Carlo's word could stop a bullet from flying or make a judge forget a body had been found.

Now it sat dark and hollow, a husk of its legacy.

Until tonight.

Salvatore stood in front of the building with Frankie and two quiet soldiers. There was no crowd. No grand speech. Just a cold wind and the sound of a gasoline can sloshing as Rico poured it along the floorboards and walls.

Frankie looked to Salvatore. "You sure?"

"I'm not sending a message," Salvatore replied. "I'm carving it into the bones of this city."

He struck the match.

The flame caught instantly—greedy, wild, and fast. Fire ate through the foundation as if it had been waiting for release.

The sky above turned orange. Flames curled into the skyline like banners.

The Vitalis didn't take the Mancini seat.

They burned it to ash.

Claudia spread a new map over the table back at the Eden—red marks, black circles, new zones.

"Territory's consolidating," she said. "Old loyalties are shifting fast. Even the silent crews are calling for meetings."

Salvatore leaned on the edge of the desk, watching the flames still burn in the distance through the window.

"You think Carlo's still in the city?" she asked.

"No," Salvatore said. "He's watching from a house in Westchester or some seaside hotel. He knows it's over. And he knows we're not coming for him—not yet."

Rico walked in, brushing ash from his coat. "Nobody from their side showed up. Not even Greco."

Salvatore nodded. "Good. Let them run."

Claudia's voice dropped. "You know this peace won't hold."

"It's not peace," Salvatore said. "It's silence. And silence is the most dangerous part of a storm."

Carlo Mancini stared out the window of his Brooklyn safe-house, face gaunt, eyes distant. The room behind him was dimly lit—books, old coats, dust-covered heirlooms from better days.

Luca Greco sat at the kitchen table, polishing a revolver.

"That fire was his coronation," Luca muttered.

Carlo didn't turn. "It was his challenge."

"He wants you to stay quiet."

"He'll regret that."

Luca raised a brow. "You want to hit him again?"

Carlo finally turned. "No. Not now. Now we plant seeds. Let him think he owns the city. Let him deal with the wolves. Let him fight ghosts and see which ones bleed."

Vincent DeMarco laughed when he saw the headline.

"Brooklyn Blaze Marks Vitali Victory."

He folded the paper and tossed it on the table. "He thinks this makes him untouchable."

His consigliere, Matteo, poured two glasses of amaro. "He's got the streets. He's got silence."

Vincent lifted the glass.

"He also just inherited every one of Mancini's enemies. And mine."

Matteo frowned. "You think he'll come after us?"

Vincent smirked. "No. Not yet."

He took a sip.

"But when he does… we'll be waiting."

Joseph slept soundly in his crib. Rosa sat nearby, sewing the hem of a shirt, humming faintly.

Salvatore watched them from the doorway.

Peace looked good on them.

Too good.

He stepped out to the kitchen and opened a bottle of wine. He didn't drink. Just stared at the glass.

He could still smell smoke in his coat.

The fire hadn't gone out.

It had only changed direction.

III

Act III

The Devil's Game

19

The Council of Five

It had once hosted foreign dignitaries and war heroes. Now, the Grand Vesey Ballroom—marbled, gilded, draped in velvet—was a battleground of a different kind. The chandeliers still sparkled like stars above a city drowning in rain. But today, they flickered over killers, kingpins, and the quiet tension of vendettas delayed.

Salvatore Vitali sat at the head of a long, polished table, flanked by Claudia on his left and Frankie on his right. Behind them stood five hand-picked soldiers—silent, stone-faced, and loyal.

Across the room, the heads of the New York's crime families filtered in like royalty arriving for war disguised as peace.

Marco Lombardi, crisp in a gray suit with a carnation on his lapel, strolled in first, smiling like the devil after confession.

Vincent DeMarco, broad-shouldered and freshly shaved,

nodded once without speaking. His consigliere, Matteo, hovered close, eyes sweeping everything.

Aldo Navarra, the eldest, walked with a cane and a stare cold enough to stop blood. His Bronx crew had taken no sides in the war, but profited from it.

Terence O'Leary, the only Irishman in the room, poured a drink before he sat. He wasn't a boss in the traditional sense, but he controlled enough East Side judges to matter more than most.

And finally, one empty chair.

Carlo Mancini's.

Salvatore glanced at it, unmoved.

He stood slowly.

"Gentlemen," he began, voice steady, measured. "We're here not because we want peace, but because we're too tired to bury more men."

A ripple of quiet agreement moved around the table.

Salvatore continued, "Each of you fought. Each of you bled. Some of you stayed in the shadows, others stepped into the fire. But now we divide the ashes—and ensure they don't catch flame again."

Lombardi leaned forward, hands folded. "And how do you propose we do that?"

Salvatore gestured to Claudia, who unfolded a large map of New York and laid it across the table. The city was divided into colored sections—each one representing territory, interest, and long-standing vendettas now frozen in ink.

"West Brooklyn and the Navy Yard remain under Vitali protection," Claudia said. "So does the Red Hook dockyard and all its routes. Lombardi holds Queens and Staten Island. DeMarco retains Upper Manhattan and the casino corridor.

Navarra keeps control of the Bronx. O'Leary keeps Manhattan courts and Irish trade corridors."

"What about Manhattan proper?" DeMarco asked. "The Midtown line?"

Salvatore met his eyes. "Neutral zone. No collections. No soldiers. Only businessmen and silence."

DeMarco snorted. "You think you can *enforce* silence?"

"I know I can," Salvatore said.

O'Leary raised a brow. "And if someone breaks that?"

"Then everyone at this table feels the knife," Claudia replied coolly. "And not in the back."

Navarra grunted. "Old rules, then."

"No," Salvatore said. "New expectations."

Thirty Minutes Later

The map became a battleground of fingers and threats. Words sharpened. Drinks spilled. Frankie stepped forward once when DeMarco raised his voice, but Salvatore waved him down.

Lombardi, ever the mediator, smiled through the chaos. "We're criminals, not children. The lines are drawn. Let's shake hands before someone loses one."

DeMarco looked to Salvatore. "And what about you? What makes you so sure you'll keep what you've taken?"

Salvatore didn't blink. "Because I already paid in blood. And I'm not finished paying."

The room quieted.

Navarra leaned back in his chair. "He's right. The boy's got the eyes of a man who buried too many to bluff."

Salvatore allowed the silence to settle before continuing.

"We'll rotate summits quarterly. One delegate per family. Any move made without this table's knowledge will be treated as an act of war. And if any one of us dies without cause—"

"—We all bleed," Lombardi finished. "Just like the old days."

"No," Salvatore said. "Better than the old days."

Claudia walked beside Salvatore in the lobby as the families began to exit in waves.

"You held the room," she said.

"I didn't need to hold it," Salvatore replied. "I needed them to look at the chair Mancini didn't sit in."

She nodded. "DeMarco's watching you too close."

"He's not watching," Salvatore said. "He's waiting."

"For what?"

Salvatore looked past her toward the city beyond the glass doors.

"For me to make a mistake."

In a private room of the Ballroom, Matteo poured two fingers of brandy for Vincent DeMarco, who swirled it slowly.

"That wasn't a summit," Vincent muttered. "It was a funeral for the old order."

"Yours?" Matteo asked.

Vincent downed the drink. "His. Sooner or later."

He stood.

"Let him play Don. Let him mark maps and pass rules."

He crushed the empty glass in his palm.

"When we come, we won't ask for permission."

Part II - Later That Night - Eden, Back Office

The map from the summit lay unrolled across the oak table, dotted with handwritten annotations from Claudia. The official division of New York was already evolving. Territory lines shifted like tide marks—fluid beneath the illusion of permanence.

Salvatore stared at it in silence.

Frankie poured a drink and passed it over. "To peace."

Salvatore didn't touch the glass.

"Peace," he said, "is just the quiet between storms."

Rico leaned in from the doorway. "We're getting feelers from Navarra's people. They want to meet, talk labor unions and freight lines."

"Navarra doesn't talk unless someone whispers first," Claudia said.

"I'll take the meeting," Salvatore replied. "See what they want."

Frankie narrowed his eyes. "You think they're looking to partner or prod?"

"Either way," Salvatore said, "we answer the same."

The next day, Joseph was playing on the floor, wooden blocks scattered in small towers. Rosa watched quietly from the armchair, sewing needle between her fingers, but unmoving.

Salvatore entered with a coat damp from the rain.

"They signed the agreement," he said. "Lombardi, Navarra, O'Leary. Even DeMarco."

Rosa didn't look up. "And?"

"And they'll break it."

She met his eyes. "When?"

"Sooner than I'd hoped."

He knelt beside Joseph, resting a hand gently on his son's back.

"I'm building something here. Not just a name. A future; for our children."

His hand fell gently on Rosa's newly pregnant torso.

"You don't build a future with men like them," Rosa said softly. "You build graves."

He said nothing.

Because he knew she was right.

In the shadows of Eden's more legitimate façade, the Vitali family ran its older operations from a quieter, older building—The Vitali Clubhouse in Bensonhurst; less glitz, more concrete.

Inside, Claudia met with two trusted lieutenants: Nico Romano and Erik Voss.

Nico had been Salvatore's pick from the early bootlegging days—a steady earner, quiet, cautious. Voss had joined during the war with Mancini—brash, brilliant with numbers, and hungry.

Too hungry.

"We're consolidating collections in Red Hook and Brighton," Claudia said. "Frankie will oversee the handoff. Salvatore wants no friction."

Nico nodded. "We'll keep it clean."

Voss leaned back in his chair. "And what do we do when DeMarco starts cutting in again? Ignore him?"

"We hold the line," Claudia replied.

Voss scoffed. "The city doesn't respect lines. It respects fire."

"Are you questioning Salvatore?" Nico asked, raising a brow.

Voss smirked. "I'm questioning silence. And I'm not the only one."

Claudia's tone turned icy. "Then you'd better make sure the ones asking questions remember who pulled this family out of the dirt."

Vincent DeMarco leafed through the list of shipping companies now flying Vitali-friendly flags.

He jabbed a finger at one name. "This used to be ours."

Matteo nodded. "They flipped after the docks."

Vincent tossed the file down. "He's not just grabbing power—he's erasing us."

Matteo poured them both coffee. "You want to make a move?"

"No," Vincent said. "We let him have the light."

Matteo raised a brow. "And we take the dark?"

Vincent smiled thinly. "Exactly."

Claudia shut the door behind her in the private office of the Eden. "We may have a leak."

Salvatore looked up. "Who?"

"Someone in operations. Numbers don't match. Voss is skimming—or someone above him is hiding it for a reason."

Salvatore leaned back in his chair. "Call him in."

"Not yet," she said. "Let me dig."

He studied her. "You trust him?"

Claudia's silence answered.

Salvatore tapped the table once, then stood.

"Tomorrow I speak to Navarra. See if his handshake means more than his silence."

"And Voss?" she asked.

"If he's loyal, he'll prove it."

"And if he's not?"

Salvatore's voice was low.

"Then we remind him where loyalty ends."

Frankie lit two cigars and handed one to Salvatore on the Eden rooftop.

"I heard Voss is sniffing around the DeMarco line."

"He's young," Salvatore said. "Wants more than he's earned."

Frankie puffed once. "He's not the first."

"No," Salvatore replied. "But he might be the last if he's not careful."

He looked across the river, the lights of Manhattan twinkling like stars from a different world.

"We gave them peace," he said. "But they don't want peace. They want a crown."

Frankie chuckled. "And they don't realize you're not holding a crown."

Salvatore turned to him.

"I'm holding the blade."

Part III - Morning - Sullivan Street Flat

Rosa brewed coffee as Salvatore tied his tie in the mirror. He looked tired, less from the war and more from what came after.

"You didn't sleep," she said.

"No," he replied. "The city sleeps. I don't."

She brought the cup to him and kissed his cheek. "Then

make sure you don't mistake silence for safety."

Salvatore met her eyes in the glass. "I don't mistake anything anymore."

Claudia stood at the chalkboard of the Vitai Clubhouse reviewing financial logs with Nico Romano.

"Everything we traced leads back to one corridor," Nico said. "A fund Voss set up for 'emergency logistics.'"

"Is it laundered?" Claudia asked.

"Barely. Sloppy. He's not hiding it. He's testing us."

She tapped her chalk twice, irritated. "Trying to prove he's untouchable."

Nico frowned. "He's wrong."

Claudia nodded. "Let Salvatore decide how wrong."

At the Eden that night, Voss sat across from Salvatore, arms crossed, eyes calculating. Behind him, Claudia stood with her arms folded, and Frankie leaned against the door, a silent wall of muscle.

"You've been creative with the books," Salvatore said without raising his voice. "Tell me why."

"I was preparing," Voss said.

"For what?"

"For when this summit collapses. For when DeMarco or Navarra or Lombardi make their move. You say you want peace, but this city's never held it longer than a breath."

Salvatore stared at him. "So you thought you'd build your own fortress?"

"I thought I'd have options."

"Options," Salvatore repeated softly, then looked to Claudia. "He's done."

Voss's confidence cracked. "You're exiling me?"

Salvatore stood. "I'm promoting you. To silence."

Frankie grabbed him by the collar. Voss shouted, "You can't build an empire without ambition!"

Salvatore stepped forward, quiet and cold.

"And I can't keep one with *yours*."

Claudia opened the door.

"Take him to Jersey. Make sure he forgets his name."

Vincent DeMarco stood at the head of his table, staring down at a street-level map of South Brooklyn.

Matteo entered quietly.

"You were right," Matteo said. "Vitali's cutting the fat."

"He thinks that makes him strong," Vincent replied.

"Then we hit now?"

Vincent shook his head. "Not yet. We let him keep cutting. By the time he realizes he's bleeding himself, we'll already have the knife at his throat."

Matteo poured a drink. "And in the meantime?"

Vincent turned to the window. "Call in the favor. Let's hurt Vitali's heart."

20

Rosa's Tragedy

Part I - Evening - Sullivan Street Flat

Rain hit the windows in gentle waves. The kind of rain Rosa loved—soft, rhythmic, cleansing. She hummed as she poured the tea, the same blend she'd sipped during her first pregnancy with Joseph. Chamomile and orange peel, honey stirred twice.

Salvatore was in the next room, speaking low into the phone. Joseph played on the rug, stacking blocks into tiny towers. Rosa smiled as she watched him.

Then, the world shifted.

A sharp, sudden pain bloomed in her gut. The teacup slipped from her hand and shattered across the tile. She clutched her stomach, breath catching as the cramp twisted deeper.

Joseph's blocks toppled.

Then she collapsed.

The St. Martha's Emergency Ward hallway lights buzzed overhead. Salvatore paced like a caged animal, tie loosened, jaw clenched. His coat was soaked from the rain and spattered with the tea stains that had dripped from Rosa's lips.

Frankie and Claudia arrived minutes later.

"Where is she?" Claudia asked.

"Inside," Salvatore said without looking up. "The baby…"

He couldn't finish the sentence.

The double doors opened, and Dr. Merullo stepped out. His face was pale, his gloves stained red.

"She's stable," he said softly. "But I'm sorry, Sal. The child…"

Salvatore didn't move. Didn't blink. Just nodded once.

"Can I see her?"

The doctor nodded.

Rosa looked small beneath the white sheets. Fragile, unlike anything Salvatore had seen before. Her hand trembled slightly when she reached for his.

"I felt it," she whispered. "Right after the first sip. A twisting. Like something inside me was fighting."

Salvatore sat beside her. "It wasn't your fault."

"I know," she said, tears welling. "But I can't help thinking…"

He squeezed her hand. "Who gave you the tea?"

"I made it myself," she said. "But the leaves—Claudia dropped them off last week. A gift from the market."

His heart froze.

He kissed her forehead and whispered, "Rest."

Then he stood, turned, and left the room without a word.

Claudia was already waiting at the Eden. Frankie stood beside her, arms crossed.

"It wasn't the leaves," Claudia said as Salvatore entered. "I had them checked the minute you called. Clean."

"Then someone swapped the tin," Salvatore said.

Frankie scowled. "Someone who knew where Rosa kept it. Or someone who got close enough to touch it."

"Someone on the inside," Claudia murmured.

"No," Salvatore said. "Someone on the *Council.*"

Frankie blinked. "You think it was one of the bosses?"

"I don't think," Salvatore replied. "I *know.*"

He stepped toward the map on the wall—the one showing each family's territory.

"There's only one way poison reaches Rosa's tea without someone noticing," he said. "It was deliberate. Personal. And symbolic."

Claudia stepped forward. "You're saying it wasn't meant to kill Rosa?"

"No," Salvatore said darkly. "It was meant to kill her. The miscarriage is just a consolation prize to whoever did it."

Frankie's voice dropped. "You think it's DeMarco?"

Salvatore stared at Upper Manhattan on the map, but didn't answer.

Not yet.

Vincent DeMarco poured a drink without ceremony. Matteo read the news aloud from the late edition:

"Vitali Family Suffers Tragedy: Rosa Vitali Hospitalized, Child Lost."

Vincent said nothing.

Matteo lowered the paper. "It worked."

Vincent sipped his whiskey. "That's the favor. That's the warning."

"You want him to know it came from us?"

"Not yet," Vincent said. "Let him drown in doubt. Let him

blame everyone before he finds the name."

He set the glass down gently.

"Sometimes the best message is the one that arrives last."

Salvatore's office at the Eden was dim, save for the desk lamp burning low. Claudia returned with a fresh report.

"The staff's clean," she said. "No one entered the flat in the last forty-eight hours but family and Frankie."

"Then it happened before that," Salvatore said.

"Or," she hesitated, "someone close was used without knowing it."

Salvatore clenched his jaw. "We've let them believe peace was real. That was our mistake."

Claudia nodded. "What now?"

Salvatore opened the drawer and pulled out the small silver revolver Barone had left him—the one from Palermo.

"Now we remind them that blood bought the table they sit at."

Part II - Morning - Eden, Salvatore's Office

The office smelled faintly of cigar smoke and varnish. Salvatore hadn't slept. He'd spent the last six hours redrawing connections—revisiting the guest list from the summit, the schedules of his lieutenants, the routes taken by his drivers. Every detail mattered now.

Claudia entered with black coffee and a crisp sheet of paper.

"This is everyone who visited the flat in the last two weeks—maid staff, delivery boys, family, council delegates."

Salvatore took it, eyes scanning fast. He tapped two names.

"Cross-check them against Navarra's people. If either was borrowed, I want to know why."

Claudia nodded. "Rosa's stable. The doctor says the worst is over."

Salvatore didn't look up. "The worst hasn't even started."

Frankie leaned on the bar of the Clubhouse, flipping a coin over his knuckles. "You really think it was Council?"

Salvatore sat across from him, arms folded, jaw tight. "This wasn't about turf. It was about legacy. Someone sent a message meant to echo through bloodlines."

Frankie frowned. "I'll check the routes for the leaf shipments. Maybe someone swapped the tin before it even reached Claudia."

"No," Salvatore said. "That tin came straight from the market. I traced the vendor myself. They've been clean for twenty years."

Frankie stared at him. "Then it had to be after."

Salvatore nodded. "Someone got close."

"Inside job?"

Salvatore's voice dropped. "Inside *Council*."

The Lombardi estate in Staten Island was gilded, overstaffed, and empty of trust. Salvatore entered with Claudia and two guards, but Lombardi insisted they speak alone.

"I heard what happened," Marco said, pouring two glasses of limoncello. "Tragedy."

Salvatore didn't drink. "I'm not here for condolences."

Marco sipped his own glass. "Then what do you want?"

"To know if your hands are clean."

Marco chuckled. "If I wanted your wife dead, I wouldn't have used tea leaves."

"Would've been louder?"

"Would've been final."

Salvatore held his gaze. "You say that like I should be comforted."

"I say that," Marco replied, "so you stop wasting time and look where the rot actually lives."

Salvatore leaned forward. "And where would you suggest I look?"

Marco grinned. "I'd start with Uptown."

Terence O'Leary wasn't a mobster in the traditional sense. He wore tweed and carried books more often than bullets. But his reach through the Irish labor courts and city clerks made him indispensable.

They walked the promenade near the East River, away from prying ears.

"You know I don't poison people," O'Leary said plainly. "It's a coward's game."

"You also don't attend summits unless your seat's threatened."

O'Leary chuckled. "Touche."

They walked in silence for a stretch.

"If it were me," O'Leary said, "I'd ask myself who benefits. And who fears an heir to your name."

Salvatore stopped walking. "You think they're afraid of my son?"

"They're afraid of what comes after you," O'Leary said. "Your name with roots. Your shadow getting longer."

He nodded toward the skyline.

"Men fear things they can't kill. Like time. Like bloodlines."

Claudia reviewed the interviews from the day. "Lombardi and O'Leary are clean, far as I can tell."

"They're arrogant," Salvatore said. "But not cowardly."

"That leaves Navarra," Claudia offered. "Or DeMarco."

Salvatore stared at the ceiling. "Navarra doesn't move unless someone pays him. DeMarco…"

Claudia finished the thought. "DeMarco's patient."

"He's also bitter," Salvatore added. "He lost ground after the docks. The summit put him at my table. But he wants the table."

Claudia laid out the notes, photographs, and one final item— a market receipt, dated two days before the poisoning.

"Look here," she said. "The vendor wrote in a note that the tea wasn't picked up by Claudia herself, but by a 'young man with a driver's cap.'"

Salvatore frowned. "We don't use drivers for pickups like that."

Claudia nodded. "Exactly."

Vincent DeMarco lit a match and let it burn low before blowing it out.

Matteo watched him in silence.

"You think he suspects?"

"He suspects *everyone*," DeMarco said. "But he's close."

Matteo raised a brow. "And when he figures it out?"

DeMarco poured a shot and downed it.

"Then we see if he values vengeance more than the empire he just built."

Part III - Early Morning - Eden, Backroom

The lights buzzed overhead as Claudia flipped through a stack of still photographs and handwritten logs. The Vitali crew had eyes on most of the blocks near Sullivan Street, with plainclothes lookouts noting anything unusual in regular reports.

"Nothing out of the ordinary," Claudia muttered, skimming the logbook. "Foot traffic normal. Regular drop-offs. No strange vehicles listed."

Salvatore leaned against the wall, arms crossed, face cold. "Go back. Afternoon of the poisoning. Read it again."

She traced her finger down the page. "Delivery boys. Fruit vendor. Sanitation truck parked too long."

"Hold there," he said.

"The truck?"

Salvatore stepped closer. "That's not city sanitation. They only do morning pickup. And that vendor—he's out of place. We don't have a fruit guy on that corner."

Claudia raised an eyebrow. "Think it was cover?"

"Check both. Vendor license. Truck plate."

She nodded. "On it."

Frankie laid a half-dozen photos across the table. "Every Council member had at least one guy in the city that week. But Navarra's men stayed close to Sunset. O'Leary's didn't leave Midtown."

Salvatore studied the photos. "DeMarco?"

Frankie slid over another envelope. "Two of his lieutenants were in Brooklyn the afternoon Rosa collapsed. One near the Fulton Market. The other—unaccounted for."

"And the sanitation truck?"

"Registered to a dummy corporation," Frankie said. "Shell company traced back to a chain of shipping operations. No known link to DeMarco, but…"

"But that means nothing," Salvatore muttered. "He's too smart to sign the paperwork himself."

He stared at the wall map again, eyes heavy.

"Who gave the order?" he whispered.

Salvatore met with Marco Lombardi in a back garden away from ears. Birds chirped over trimmed hedges. The contrast with his mood was surreal.

"You've come to check my pockets again?" Marco asked, mock insulted.

"I'm checking shadows," Salvatore said. "You don't mind, do you?"

Marco smirked. "Not if it brings you clarity."

Salvatore narrowed his eyes. "Have you heard anything?"

Marco sipped his espresso. "Only that you're shaking every tree that ever looked in your direction."

"Shouldn't I?"

"Oh, you should," Marco said, gaze darkening. "Just remember—some branches snap back."

Rico returned that evening, looking half-soaked in rain and half-pissed.

"Been asking quiet questions," he said. "Had a contact check call logs."

"And?" Salvatore asked.

"Police were on Sullivan Street the afternoon Rosa collapsed. No call from the flat. No incident report. No arrests."

Salvatore stiffened. "Why were they there?"
"No one knows," Rico said. "But they were there."
Salvatore's mind raced. "Uniformed?"
"Plainclothes," Rico said. "Two of them. Names aren't listed."
"Cops don't visit without a reason."
Rico nodded. "And if they didn't file anything…"
"Then they weren't just cops."

Claudia joined Salvatore under the slate-gray sky. The city glowed beneath a curtain of mist.
"We're close," she said.
"No," Salvatore replied. "We're circling. And someone's staying just out of reach."
"Who?"
He stared toward Queens.
"I don't know yet."
He turned to her.
"But I will."

21

O'Hara's Last Breath

Part I - Morning - Lower Manhattan, Precinct Records
Room

The smell of damp paper and cigarette smoke hung heavy in
the file room, even with the door propped open. Claudia stood
beside a rusted cabinet, flipping through yellowing manila
folders. Rico stood guard near the entrance, watching the
hallway like a coiled spring.

Salvatore, unshaven and tense, rifled through a stack of
internal memos tied to plainclothes patrols.

"There," Claudia said, tapping a folder. "Unscheduled
plainclothes detail. Sullivan Street. Logged under community
outreach."

Salvatore scanned the names.

"Detective Sergeant Patrick O'Hara. Partner listed as 'C.
Jones'—alias. Not a real cop."

Claudia frowned. "You think O'Hara knew?"

"I think he let it happen," Salvatore said, teeth clenched.

"And probably more."

He pulled out another file—an internal complaint from a year earlier: O'Hara seen in a known trouble spot in Jackson Heights. No follow-up. No discipline.

Rico stepped in. "O'Hara's been quiet since the summit. But someone said he's been keeping his head low."

Salvatore nodded slowly.

"O'Hara doesn't hide unless there's guilt."

He slammed the cabinet shut.

"Bring him in. Quietly."

Rain pattered gently on the windows of the Eden as the room sat heavy in silence. Frankie leaned against the doorframe as Claudia laid out the logistics of what Salvatore had ordered. A public message. A warning to every man who wore a badge or carried a debt.

"No blood in the alley," Claudia said. "We do this where they all can see it."

Salvatore looked up from the table. "Where?"

"The square off Mulberry," she said. "One of ours is cleaning up the scaffolding. We'll set a crate stage—no guns drawn. Put on a show and a warning."

Frankie folded his arms. "You sure this is the right move? The families will see it. Some might call it reckless."

Salvatore stood. "Let them. Let them all see what happens when my family is touched."

He nodded to Rico. "Get O'Hara. Dress him. No bruises. I want him standing upright until the last second."

The crowd gathered fast. Word had traveled by whispers and glances. No name had been spoken, but everyone knew someone was going to die. And they all wanted to see who.

Streetlights cast orange halos as Eden's men worked quickly. A makeshift stage was hammered into place—a shipping crate raised on pallets. Two black folding chairs. One for the condemned. One for the judge.

By the time the car rolled up, the square was full. Men from all five boroughs—runners, capos, bagmen, lookouts. Faces familiar and strange watched from doorways and alleys. The kind of silence that meant memory.

O'Hara was pulled from the backseat. His eyes were wide, lips dry. No fight left. Just confusion.

"Sal," he muttered as he was led to the platform. "I didn't know. I swear to God—"

Salvatore climbed the crate steps slowly. Claudia waited at the base, arms crossed.

The city held its breath.

"You wore a badge," Salvatore said, voice loud enough to cut through the wind. "You took a bribe. You opened a door. And when they came for my family, you let them walk in."

O'Hara's knees buckled. He looked out at the crowd. "I didn't—"

"You were there," Salvatore said. "That's enough."

He turned away, back straight, the weight of judgment already in motion. He stepped off the stage and into the shadows.

The spectacle was complete; Salvatore was smart enough to know not to kill a cop in broad daylight. But that would change as the sun went down.

Part II - Evening - Mulberry Square

It started like any other evening in Lower Manhattan. Foot traffic thinned as businesses closed, and the usual hum of the streets softened under the fading light. But something was off. The air was tense. Familiar faces appeared where they didn't usually linger. Cigarettes burned slower. Conversations were shorter. Eyes were alert.

O'Hara walked alone, blending into the bustle of the square in his long brown coat and newsboy cap pulled low. He didn't know he was being followed. He was trying his best to escape the city.

He passed a fruit stand. A man pretending to haggle watched him. At the bakery, a delivery boy tracked his stride. In a second-story window across the street, a silhouette shifted behind a curtain.

O'Hara kept moving, heading toward the train entrance. He never made it.

A sharp crack echoed through the square.

It didn't sound like much at first—more like a car backfiring. But people near the sound turned quickly. Then they saw the body.

O'Hara lay face down in the gutter, blood blooming across his shoulder and pooling beneath his head. One hand was still clutching his coat as if trying to keep it wrapped around him. His cap had rolled into the street.

No one screamed. No one ran.

They'd seen this before. They knew the rules.

A few people crossed themselves. A man at the corner whispered a name that never made it to the police.

There had been no declaration. No warning. Just the

moment, and then the absence.

The shooter—Enzo Silvano—was already gone. A nondescript coat, a hidden pistol, a practiced stride. He was absorbed by the crowd within moments. No one remembered his face. Just the fact that someone had walked up behind O'Hara and ended a chapter.

Within minutes, the police arrived. They cordoned off the area, asked empty questions, filed hollow reports.

By then, every paperboy in the district already knew the headline.

"DIRTY COP FOUND DEAD IN MULBERRY SQUARE"

At a bar in Red Hook, two bartenders argued about whether it had been a mob hit or a personal vendetta. A man in a suit quietly slid his drink forward and said, "It was justice."

Another nodded. "The badge doesn't make you holy."

Someone else muttered, "The badge got him killed."

The arguments didn't matter. The result did. Everyone understood the rules had changed. No more protection. No more illusions.

Claudia lit a cigarette and exhaled toward the sky on the Eden rooftop. The wind took the smoke, but it didn't clear the weight pressing on her chest.

"He's dead," she said softly.

Salvatore stood a few paces away, watching the streetlights flicker far below.

"Good," he said, barely audible.

"They'll talk," she continued. "They'll say it was you, even if you weren't there."

"I wasn't supposed to be," Salvatore replied. "The death

wasn't the show. It was the warning."

She took a long drag. "He didn't give us a name."

"He gave us permission," Salvatore said. "That's all I needed."

They stood in silence for a long moment.

Claudia looked over. "Do you think the message landed?"

Salvatore nodded slowly. "They'll find the blood. They'll read between the lines. And they'll know one thing."

"What's that?"

"That the next one might not get the mercy of a quick end.

Part III - The Next Morning - DeMarco Clubhouse

Vincent DeMarco sat at the far end of a long mahogany table, one hand wrapped around a crystal glass of Sicilian red, the other tapping thoughtfully on the wood. Matteo stood near the fireplace, holding a folded copy of that morning's newspaper. The headline ran in thick black ink:

"Disgraced Officer Slain in Mob-Style Execution"

Matteo unfolded it fully, revealing a grainy photo of O'Hara's body sprawled in the street, half-shrouded by a white sheet. Blood had soaked into the gutter like spilled wine.

DeMarco chuckled and lifted his glass. "To Salvatore Vitali—bringer of justice, punisher of ghosts."

Matteo didn't smile. "He thinks he's struck a blow."

"He has," DeMarco said, swirling the wine. "But not at the right man."

Matteo walked to the window, peering out at the gray skyline of Queens. "You knew he'd go after O'Hara."

"I counted on it," DeMarco replied. "He was sloppy. Guilty. He gave Salvatore just enough to satisfy his rage—but not enough to unravel anything real."

"Still," Matteo said, "public execution of a cop. It rattled people."

"Good," DeMarco said. "Let them be rattled. Let them think Salvatore's lost his restraint. The more reckless he looks, the easier it is to isolate him."

He finished the glass and set it down gently.

"It's time."

Matteo turned from the window. "You want to bring him back?"

DeMarco nodded. "We need someone who knows Salvatore. Someone who's close—but angry. Someone he trusted once."

Matteo didn't speak for a long moment. "You really think he'll flip?"

"I don't need him to flip," DeMarco said. "I just need him to show Salvatore something he doesn't want to see."

The man stood over a dusty suitcase, slowly pulling out a photograph. In it, a much younger Salvatore Vitali grinned alongside him, arms slung over shoulders, laughter frozen in time. The other man's eyes were harder now. Older. Worn.

Aldo Rossi.

Ex-partner. Ex-friend. Ex-Vitali.

Banished after the Mancini leak fallout. Silenced, but never truly gone.

Matteo waited at the kitchen table. "You heard?"

"I heard," Aldo said, staring at the photo. "O'Hara's dead."

"Salvatore made it personal."

Aldo snorted. "It's always personal with him."

Matteo leaned forward. "He still thinks you're rotting down south."

"I was," Aldo said. "Until you called."

"We want you in."

Aldo turned slowly, his voice careful. "You don't want me in. You want me *close* to him."

Matteo didn't deny it.

"You know what he did to me?" Aldo asked.

"I know you were loyal. And I know he cast you out."

Aldo tossed the photo onto the table. "He didn't just cast me out. He buried me.

"Did it?"

Aldo shrugged. "Doesn't matter anymore, does it?"

"No," Matteo said. "Only what happens next."

Aldo poured himself a drink. "What happens next is… I make him look in the mirror. And I make sure he doesn't like what he sees."

Salvatore stood in front of the city map in his Eden office, the pins and red strings like arteries of control. Claudia entered, her arms crossed.

"The street's quiet. No retaliation. No whispers from the Council."

"They're waiting," Salvatore said. "Everyone's waiting."

"For what?"

"For me to crack."

She raised an eyebrow. "And are you?"

Salvatore turned, eyes bloodshot but steady. "No. But I am starting to wonder."

"About what?"

He exhaled. "Why the silence feels louder than the blood."

DeMarco sat in the backseat, watching the skyline, a soft classical record humming from the radio.

Matteo lit a cigarette.

"Aldo's on the move," he said.

"Good."

"You think he'll turn?" Matteo asked.

"No," DeMarco said with a grin. "But he'll force Salvatore to."

"To what?"

"To remember what he buried."

Aldo stood alone beneath a flickering lamppost near the Brooklyn Docks, staring out over the dark water.

He ran a thumb across the crease in the photo—the one from the Havana smuggling haul, the last time he and Salvatore smiled at the same table.

He hadn't come back for revenge.

He'd come back to finish what had been left unfinished.

22

The Ballad of Aldo Rossi

Part I - Early Morning - Vitali Safehouse, East Williamsburg

Salvatore Vitali woke to silence.

The kind that doesn't hum, doesn't breathe. The kind that meant something was wrong.

He was already dressed before his boots hit the floor.

Across the room, Claudia emerged from a back hallway, gun in hand.

"Something's off," she said.

Salvatore nodded. "Doors?"

"Secured. But the lookouts haven't checked in."

Salvatore walked to the steel shutters and peeled one open slightly. The alley below was empty. Not silent—there was still a wind, a distant siren, a barking dog—but empty in the wrong way.

Frankie entered next.

Salvatore looked to Claudia. "Pull the backups."

She was already moving. Within seconds, the room buzzed. Nothing.

Salvatore exhaled slowly.

"They want us nervous."

The crew had assembled quickly. Frankie. Claudia. Rico. A few trusted lieutenants. All armed, all wary. They formed a tight circle in the garage below the safehouse, lit only by a swinging bulb overhead.

"Still no word from the outside?" Salvatore asked.

Claudia shook her head. "Like they vanished. Phones dead. Runners gone. I've never seen it this quiet."

"It's a trap," Frankie said flatly.

"It's a message," Salvatore corrected. "Someone wants me boxed in. Pushed to react."

"What's the play?" Claudia asked.

Salvatore looked around the room. "We don't run. We wait."

"For what?" Rico muttered.

Salvatore turned to the garage door. "For whoever's brave—or stupid—enough to walk through that door."

The silence was broken only by the sound of dripping water echoing through the tunnels beneath Eden. Salvatore moved quickly now, flanked by Claudia and Frankie, using one of the emergency exits few even knew existed. It was clear the safehouse had been compromised.

Claudia had confirmed it minutes earlier—one of the guards had been found slumped in a stairwell, neck broken. No gunfire. No struggle. A professional job.

Salvatore hated the idea of fleeing. But he wasn't about to be boxed in.

They emerged into the back hallway of Eden, the club still closed, the floors half-lit by emergency backup power.

Frankie secured the exits while Claudia swept the office upstairs. Salvatore poured a glass of water and leaned against the bar, eyes narrowed.

"They're circling me like dogs."

"Not dogs," Claudia said from the staircase. "Hyenas. Smiling. Waiting for the first drop of blood."

Salvatore downed the water.

"Then I'll bleed them first."

Elsewhere, Aldo Rossi stared at a black-and-white photo of Salvatore taken the night before. He set it down beside several others—images of Vitali lieutenants, routes, safehouse doors.

Matteo entered behind him.

"You ready?"

Aldo didn't answer right away.

"Don't underestimate him," Matteo warned.

"I never have."

Matteo studied Aldo's profile. "You still planning to talk to him first?"

Aldo nodded. "If he listens."

"And if he doesn't?"

Aldo turned, his expression hard. "Then we finish it the way this life always ends."

Part II - Morning – Sullivan Street Flat

Rosa sat by the window, her eyes unfocused, hands folded tightly in her lap. She hadn't spoken much since the incident. Her grief, sharper than any knife, had cooled into something more solid, like marble around the soul. Salvatore poured her tea silently and took the chair across from her.

"They're watching us," she said suddenly, eyes still fixed on the street below.

"Who?" Salvatore asked.

"Everyone."

He didn't deny it. "That's the price of wearing the crown."

"No," Rosa said. "It's the price of becoming the reason everyone else wants one."

She looked at him. "They'll come at you through everything you love."

"I know."

Rosa set the cup down, untouched. "Then whatever happens next, make sure you survive it. I can live without peace. I won't live without you."

Frankie tossed a file down on the Eden office table. "Aldo Rossi's name started floating around again."

Claudia raised an eyebrow. "That's impossible. He's been in exile. for years."

Frankie shrugged. "Yeah? Well someone's seen a man matching his description at two separate places tied to DeMarco's shipping lanes."

"Salvatore banished him five years ago," Claudia said. "After he sold out to the Mancinis."

"He's not supposed to be in the city," Frankie said. "But he is."

Claudia turned to Salvatore. "What do you want to do?"

Salvatore didn't hesitate. "Bring him in."

"Alive?"

"For now."

Aldo sat across from Matteo, sipping black coffee.

"He knows I'm in town," Aldo said.

"That was the point," Matteo replied. "He'll come for you."

"You still haven't told me the full play."

Matteo leaned forward. "You don't need to know it all. Just make sure only one of you is able to leave the meeting alive."

"And then?"

"Then you disappear again."

Aldo scoffed. "I didn't come back just to run."

"You came back because you hate what he became."

Aldo looked away. "I came back because he turned his back on me. For one mistake."

The Vitali crew tailed the sightings until a single consistent lead surfaced: an old cold storage depot once used during the Mancini era, now reactivated under a shell company with quiet ties to DeMarco's logistics network.

Salvatore, Frankie, and Claudia arrived after nightfall. They moved through the alley silently, weapons drawn but hidden.

Inside, only a single desk lamp lit the otherwise empty interior.

Aldo was waiting.

He stood calm, hands visible, eyes locked on the man who had once been his brother in blood.

"Took you long enough," Aldo said.

Salvatore stepped into the light.

"You've got a lot of nerve."

"I've got something better," Aldo replied. "Memory."

Claudia and Frankie fanned out behind Salvatore, covering the angles.

"You were told never to show your face here again."

"Yeah," Aldo said. "But I figured with everything going on, maybe you'd want to hear my side."

"There's no side to betrayal."

"Is that what you tell yourself?" Aldo snapped. "I didn't betray you, Sal. I was desperate. The Mancinis were circling. I made a deal to protect what we built."

"You made a deal to protect *yourself.*"

"You left me no choice!"

Salvatore's tone dropped to ice. "We always have a choice. You chose the enemy."

Aldo stepped forward. "And you chose exile over understanding. I've lived with it. But you? You've been lied to ever since."

He tossed a folder to the ground. Inside: manifests, shipping ledgers, and notes showing forged records—courtesy of DeMarco's front companies.

"You're being boxed in," Aldo said. "And the people doing it are using the same paths we built. I helped build them. I know where they lead."

Salvatore looked down at the documents, then back up.

"And now what? You want forgiveness?"

Aldo shook his head. "I want you to know who your real enemies are."

Part III - Late Evening - Brooklyn, Cold Storage Depot

Salvatore stared across the concrete floor at the man he once called brother. The silence between them stretched long enough to pull the air from the room. Around them, the chill of refrigeration lingered, clinging to the bones.

"I should kill you for what you did," Salvatore said, voice low.

"You should," Aldo replied. "I thought you would."

Frankie tightened his grip on the pistol at his side. Claudia stood motionless, eyes flicking from one man to the other.

"I didn't come here to beg," Aldo continued. "I came here because you deserve to know what they made of us."

Salvatore took a step forward. "What are you talking about?"

"You still think it was just me who turned on you," Aldo said. "But I wasn't the first. And I wasn't the last."

Salvatore's eyes narrowed. "Start talking."

Aldo exhaled. "Everything that's happened since the Havana pipeline—Ferri, O'Hara, even me being in the city—it was all pushed forward by the same hand."

"DeMarco?" Claudia asked.

Aldo nodded. "He's been playing you for years. He saw how the Council treated you after Mancini fell. He knew if he could isolate you—make you strike out in the dark—you'd undo yourself."

Salvatore didn't speak.

"He didn't hire Ferri," Aldo continued. "Ferri was a lone blade—paranoid, dangerous. But DeMarco fed him the names. Rosa. Joseph. He pointed Ferri like a dagger and let him loose."

Claudia stepped forward. "And O'Hara?"

Aldo nodded. "Paid off. Gave access. DeMarco's people

needed an open door. O'Hara left it unlocked."

Salvatore's fists clenched. "You knew this and didn't come forward?"

Aldo's face twisted. "You exiled me, Sal. You cut me off from the only family I had. You think I didn't want to run back and tell you everything?"

"Then why now?"

"Because DeMarco's not done," Aldo said. "And whatever he has planned next—it's already moving."

Frankie paced near the back wall, agitated. "What are you saying?"

"I'm saying we've all been pieces on his board," Aldo said. "You think this ends with me? With O'Hara? No. He's still got one hand left to play."

Salvatore stepped forward until he was inches from Aldo. "What hand?"

"I don't know," Aldo admitted. "But whatever it is, it's aimed at your legacy. At the name you're trying to protect."

Salvatore's eyes narrowed. "You expect me to believe this is remorse?"

Aldo met his gaze without blinking. "No. I expect you to believe I hate DeMarco more than I hate you. He used me. He wanted me to kill you tonight. He turned me into the villain in your story."

"You did that yourself," Claudia snapped.

Aldo didn't argue. "Maybe I did. But at least now you know who pulled the strings."

A long silence passed.

Finally, Salvatore looked to Frankie. "Let him go."

Frankie hesitated. "Boss—"

"Let him go."

Aldo nodded once, slowly. "Watch your back, Sal. Whatever's coming… it won't come with noise. It'll come like a whisper. In the dark."

He turned and disappeared into the shadows of the depot.

Claudia stepped beside Salvatore. "You believe him?"

"I believe we've been looking at the wrong threats," Salvatore said. "And that the last hand is already in motion."

He stared out into the night.

"Time to reshuffle the board."

23

The Irish Betrayal

Part I - Early Morning - DeMarco's Clubhouse

The whiskey bottle slammed against the wall, shattering into a thousand shards. Vincent DeMarco stood in the center of his office, red-faced and seething.

"He let him live!" he roared. "He let that son of a bitch walk out of there breathing!"

Matteo stayed quiet, standing near the door with his arms crossed. He knew better than to interrupt when DeMarco was like this.

"All Aldo had to do was put a bullet in him," DeMarco snapped. "That was the deal. You get close, you kill Salvatore, and I bury the past. Instead, he shows up at my door last night like nothing happened—tells me he warned him!"

"He still gave us something," Matteo said carefully. "Vitali's stirred the hornet's nest. He's paranoid, bleeding men. We've got the Irish crew ready."

DeMarco sneered. "Then let O'Leary loose. Tell him no

more restraint. Burn it all. Burn everything with a Vitali name on it. No quarter, no subtlety. Make it biblical."

The scent of gun oil and old wood lingered in the Sullivan Street study as Salvatore stared out the window, coffee cooling beside him. The skyline was still bruised by the last storm, the gray light crawling over rooftops like a warning. Frankie entered, coat soaked from the rain, his face grim.

"They moved last night."

Salvatore didn't turn. "How bad?"

"Two of our crews hit. Boyle Street burned. Cosenza's place—they left a body in the doorway. Young Carlo. Shot in the back of the head."

Salvatore finally turned. "Irish?"

Frankie nodded. "O'Leary's people. But this wasn't just muscle flexing. It was scorched earth. They hit half a dozen of our spots inside four hours."

"DeMarco."

"Word is he's furious. Aldo showing his face again—he sees it as betrayal. Personal. He gave the Irish the green light to hit everything we've got. Clubs, fronts, trucks. Total war."

Salvatore's jaw clenched. "Then we hit back harder."

The tables of the Eden had been cleared, curtains drawn. Every remaining Vitali lieutenant sat in a wide circle, guarded by two men each. Salvatore stood in the center, Claudia at his side, her eyes scanning for dissent before it could form.

"They came through the dark," Salvatore began. "Lit our houses. Bled our people. Not because we were weak. Because they're afraid we're strong again."

He paced slowly, letting the weight of the room settle.

"DeMarco's made his move. He's using O'Leary's Irish dogs to do it. Hiding behind them. But make no mistake—this is his war."

He stopped and pointed at the map laid out before them.

"I say we make it his grave."

A murmur of agreement swept the room.

Claudia laid out maps and assignments.

"O'Leary's using bars along Myrtle as staging points. Two crews are holed up in a rail depot off Broadway Junction. They've got muscle from Uptown—courtesy of DeMarco."

"We hit them first," Salvatore said. "Hard. Quiet. No survivors."

Rico, one of the last old-guard enforcers, raised his voice. "And the rest of Brooklyn?"

Salvatore's gaze darkened. "Then we remind them who we were."

The first strike came at sunset at an abandoned foundry near the Gowanus Canal. A two-car team led by Claudia hit the depot along the canal, catching the Irish by surprise. The air filled with gunfire and the sharp echo of shouts in Gaelic.

Three were down in the first thirty seconds. Claudia moved like smoke through the shadows, two silenced pistols clearing the south wing. By the time backup arrived, the place was burning.

Across the borough, other teams struck the watering holes O'Leary's people had claimed. By midnight, four locations had fallen. The word spread fast—Vitali wasn't dead.

And Brooklyn wasn't for sale.

Part II - Pre-Dawn - Williamsburg Railyard

The fog rolled over the gravel like a veil. Freight cars sat idle, rusted and crooked, forming makeshift barricades. The Irish crew, clad in mismatched jackets and rain-slick boots, moved like ghosts between the boxcars.

Terence O'Leary stood on the south platform, binoculars pressed to his face. His beard was thick, his temper thicker. Behind him, Seamus carried a satchel of homemade explosives.

"We should've hit them sooner," Seamus muttered.

Connor didn't respond. He just kept watching the skyline. "DeMarco wants it all. No pieces. Just ash."

"And if Vitali pushes back?"

"Then we push harder."

Claudia circled the map like a hawk in the Eden back room, now a war room.

"They're staging at the railyard. Our intel's solid—sixteen men, half armed with automatics, two snipers, maybe more in the shadows. And Terence himself."

Salvatore folded his arms. "We can't let them dig in. This becomes a siege, we lose the borough."

Frankie cracked his knuckles. "We take the fight to them."

"No," Salvatore said. "We do it clean. Fast. Loud only at the end. We ghost their shadows."

He looked at Claudia. "Assemble the tunnel crew. We hit the yard from below."

Claudia led the strike team in silence at sunrise, each man stepping over the tracks like they were crossing into legend.

Salvatore brought up the rear, pistol holstered and a blade strapped to his wrist.

"Two exits," Claudia whispered. "We pop near the generator room and fan west. Frankie's team comes in from the old coal shaft."

"And the rest?" Salvatore asked.

"We clean house."

Terence was halfway through a cigarette when the lights went out.

"What the—?"

Then came the muffled thumps beneath the floorboards.

"Underneath!" one of his men shouted. Too late.

The first blast tore through the generator shed, sending concrete and steel flying. Claudia's team rose from the smoke, guns blazing. Seamus caught a round to the throat before he could unclip his satchel.

Frankie emerged from the east, shotgun roaring. The Irish fired back in a blind panic, but they were pinned, outflanked, and outnumbered.

Terence scrambled to higher ground, rifle in hand, but found Salvatore waiting at the top of the stairs.

"You should've stayed in Hell's Kitchen," Salvatore said.

Terence fired.

Salvatore ducked, rolled, and was on him before the second shot cleared the chamber. His blade flashed once, twice.

Terence staggered, dropped his rifle, and slumped to the metal grate.

"Brooklyn," Salvatore muttered, "belongs to the living."

The survivors trickled in by noon at the Eden. One by one,

bloodied and soot-covered but standing. Claudia tossed a bag onto the table—it landed with a heavy, wet thump.

"O'Leary's insignia," she said. "Cut it off him myself."

Frankie poured two fingers of whiskey and handed it to Salvatore. "To the dead."

Salvatore raised his glass. "To what we protect."

The toast was silent. The war wasn't over.

But Brooklyn still burned in their colors.

Part III - Late Afternoon - Eden, Rooftop

The smoke of the railyard had cleared, but Brooklyn still stank of blood and gunpowder. Salvatore stood alone, the wind tugging at his coat, the city stretched out like a battered chessboard. Below, Eden bustled—cleanup crews, wounded men patched up, weapons reloaded.

Claudia stepped onto the roof behind him. "Navarra's people sent word. They're listening."

Salvatore didn't turn. "And Lombardi?"

"Wary. But open. They know what DeMarco's doing. And they know he's not playing by the rules."

He turned to her, eyes sharp. "Set the meet. Neutral ground. I'm not asking them for help. Just room."

The old cathedral in Lower Manhattan was cold and dark, candles flickering from cracked holders. Salvatore walked the aisle in silence, footsteps echoing off stone and stained glass. At the altar, two men waited.

Marco Lombardi—dark-haired and solemn. And Angelo

Navarra—lean, wiry, with the gaze of a man who never blinked.

"You called us here," Lombardi said. "Let's not waste words."

Salvatore nodded. "We all know what DeMarco's doing. He's using outsiders to stir the pot. He plays both sides of the table and sits in the dark while we bleed."

Navarra gave a thin smile. "Sounds like DeMarco."

"I'm not asking for backup," Salvatore said. "I'm asking for silence. A freeze. I want you to turn your backs on him. Shut him out. No business. No deals. No warnings."

Lombardi raised an eyebrow. "You want us to cut off a man who still holds a seat?"

"He's already declared himself above it," Salvatore said. "He's broken rules we used to die to protect. If we keep pretending he's still one of us, he'll hollow out everything we built."

Navarra folded his hands. "You planning to kill him?"

"Yes."

Neither man flinched.

Lombardi said, "You realize what this means. If he catches wind of our silence, he'll turn on us too."

Salvatore nodded. "That's why I'll make it quick."

The silence lingered a beat too long. Then Navarra leaned forward.

"You don't owe us tribute. You don't owe us blood. But if you bring DeMarco down, make sure the world knows who did it. Loud and clear."

Salvatore extended a hand. "Then we have an understanding?"

Lombardi and Navarra each took it.

"No warnings," Lombardi said. "No aid."

"No safe harbor," Navarra added. "DeMarco's on his own."

Frankie stared at the war room table. "So they gave us the green light?"

"Not quite," Claudia said. "They gave us the silence we needed. DeMarco's frozen out."

Salvatore rolled up the map slowly. "Then we move. No more waiting. We strike the heart before he builds a new shield."

Frankie lit a cigarette. "You think he knows?"

"He will," Salvatore said. "But by the time he figures it out, it'll be too late."

He walked out, not looking back.

The war had taken brothers, sons, and saints. But the last hand was his to play.

24

The Wolf in Winter

Part I - Early Morning - DeMarco's Private Estate

The garden was silent save for the soft hiss of sprinklers and the wind shifting through the hedges. Vincent DeMarco stood beneath the arbor, bathrobe cinched tight, espresso steaming in one hand, newspaper in the other.

The front page bore the names of the dead: Terence O'Leary, Seamus O'Leary, and a half dozen others wiped from Brooklyn in one night. He read it slowly. Then again.

"You see it yet?" he said without looking up.

Matteo stepped into the light. "They're closing ranks. Lombardi. Navarra. Even the independents. Everyone's quiet."

DeMarco folded the paper. "Which means they're choosing silence over loyalty."

"They know what's coming."

"No," DeMarco said. "They think they do."

He set the espresso down and turned toward the house.

"Call the last of our people. I want the fortified spots tightened. Tell my nephew Nico to pull anything we can out of Manhattan. If Salvatore's coming, he's coming soon."

Matteo hesitated. "You think he'll really do it? Risk everything?"

DeMarco smiled faintly. "He has no choice. And he'll burn the whole board trying to get to me."

The map in the Eden war room was gone. In its place, a single black folder lay on the table. Salvatore stood behind it, arms crossed.

"We move in three days."

Frankie leaned forward. "We've never hit a man in his own fortress. DeMarco's place is shielded like a fort—stone walls, two layers of gate, and guards with automatics."

Claudia remained still. "He'll expect us to come at night. We don't. We hit at noon. When he thinks we're planning."

Salvatore opened the folder. Inside: floorplans, personnel rosters, access routes.

"He's got weakness in his maintenance line. We have someone on the inside. A groundskeeper. He'll leave the east side utility corridor unlocked. We move through the undercellar, bypass the front."

Frankie nodded slowly. "And after?"

"We kill DeMarco. Fast. Clean. The kind of kill that ends conversations."

Claudia tilted her head. "You sure they won't come after us once he's gone?"

"They might," Salvatore said. "But by then, the board will be reset."

Nico paced the length of the tiny apartment in Red Hook. His jaw was tight, his eyes bloodshot.

"They're coming, aren't they?" he asked.

Matteo stood in the corner, arms folded. "They are. And your uncle says we hold."

"Hold with what? We've lost half our crews. The Commission's turned their backs. He's blind, Matteo."

Matteo moved slowly toward the window. "Your uncle's many things. Blind isn't one of them."

Nico grabbed a pack of cigarettes. "Then he's lying to himself."

Matteo didn't argue. He just looked at the skyline.

"They'll be here before the week's out."

Nico nodded. "Then let's make them bleed for every inch."

Part II - Afternoon - Eden, Upper Office

The blinds were shut tight. The air was thick with smoke, tension, and the low murmur of preparation. Salvatore stood at the center of the room, surrounded by his top lieutenants.

Claudia unrolled a new map on the table, this one hand-drawn with red pencil and ink—every inch of DeMarco's estate, every known sentry position, every blind spot.

"There's a utility corridor on the east side," she said. "The groundskeeper we flipped will leave the latch unsecured and kill the backup light for twelve minutes. That's our window."

Salvatore nodded. "Once we're inside?"

"We sweep the lower service halls and come up near the solarium," Frankie answered. "From there, we split. Two go to lock down the east wing, the rest follow Sal to the study. That's where DeMarco'll be."

"What if he's not?" asked Luigi, one of the newer enforcers.

Salvatore's eyes were cold. "Then we burn the house down and wait for him to crawl out."

That evening, weapons were cleaned, distributed, tested. Rows of sidearms, modified shotguns, and short-barrel rifles lay glistening under the overhead lights. Claudia personally checked every suppressor.

Frankie sat with a younger soldier, going over hand signals for room clearing. "You don't shoot unless you have a line. Don't hesitate, but don't panic."

"Got it," the kid said, nervously adjusting his vest.

In the corner, Salvatore examined a vintage revolver.

Claudia approached. "That the one you took off Mancini?"

He nodded. "Thought it might bring closure."

She smiled grimly. "Fitting."

Matteo stood in the DeMarco command room, eyeing the estate's blueprints and personnel plans. Nico leaned against the wall, chewing a toothpick, watching the slow rotations of armed guards in the gardens.

"They'll come through the east," Nico said. "If they're smart."

"They're smart," Matteo said.

"So we choke them there. Mine the path, gas traps, fallback positions."

Matteo shook his head. "No mines. If we make it too loud, the other families will think we're panicking."

Nico grunted. "Then we bleed 'em slow."

Final assignments were handed out in the war room. Salvatore gave his lieutenants their routes, their timings, their dead drops. All coordination would be hand-delivered and marked in coded chalk.

"Once we go in, there's no retreat," Salvatore said. "We finish it, or we don't come back."

One of the soldiers asked, "You think he knows we're coming?"

"I hope he does," Salvatore replied. "I want him wide awake when the storm hits."

The final meeting took place at a dockside warehouse, isolated and cold. Salvatore's most trusted inner circle sat around a steel table under a single hanging bulb.

"We strike tomorrow," he said.

Frankie nodded. "Everyone's in position. The groundskeeper's been silent, but we've got the signal."

Claudia placed a leather pouch on the table. Inside were photos—DeMarco's remaining captains, known strongholds, and key loyalists.

"We hit him, we need to make sure no one fills the vacuum," she said. "We end this surgically."

Salvatore picked up one of the photos—DeMarco, younger, standing beside Mancini.

"This ends where it began."

He set the photo down and stood.

"Tomorrow, we put him in the ground."

Part III - Late Night - Sullivan Street Flat

The house was still. Outside, the city murmured with the distant groan of sirens and the hum of traffic, but within these walls, time seemed suspended.

Salvatore stood in the kitchen, sleeves rolled up, hands curled around a glass of water that had long since gone warm. He didn't drink. He just stared through it.

Rosa entered quietly, her steps soft. She wore a silk robe and the weight of years etched gently into her eyes. She didn't speak right away. Just stood beside him and laid a hand on his wrist.

"I heard," she said.

Salvatore nodded. "It's tomorrow."

Rosa leaned against the counter, facing him. "You've planned it all?"

"Every corridor. Every angle. If the gates open, he won't leave alive."

"And if they don't?"

He smiled faintly. "Then we break them."

Rosa studied him for a long moment. "Is it revenge, Sal? Or survival?"

"Both," he admitted. "But it's more than that. It's legacy. Joseph's name will never mean anything if we leave it buried beneath DeMarco's lies."

She nodded slowly. "Our son deserves more than blood in the ledger."

Salvatore turned to her. "If I don't come back—"

"Don't," Rosa interrupted. "You come back. And if you don't, you make sure they remember why they were afraid of you."

He looked away, then back. "Do you ever regret it? Any of

this?"

Rosa sighed. "Regret? Sometimes. But not the choice. You gave us a kingdom. And now it's time to defend it."

Salvatore stepped forward, taking both her hands.

He kissed her hands and held her gaze.

"Then tomorrow, I finish it."

Rosa nodded. "Then go. End it. And come back to me."

Outside, the wind picked up. Morning wasn't far.

And neither was the storm.

25

Blood on the Stone

Part I - Mid-Morning - Long Island, DeMarco's Estate Perimeter

The sun had not yet peaked, but the ground shimmered with heat and anticipation. A slow, dry wind kicked up leaves along the high stone walls of Vincent DeMarco's private estate, a fortress more than a home.

From behind the hedges and trees that surrounded the compound, dark shapes moved silently—Salvatore's men, dressed in muted coats, crouched low and tight, weapons ready.

Claudia checked her watch. "Three minutes."

Salvatore knelt beside her. The soil was dry beneath his boots, the breath between them short and calm.

"We move on my signal," he said.

A courier—one of the young runners—appeared from behind the treeline, breathless and pale. "The groundskeeper gave the signal. East gate's open."

Salvatore nodded and dismissed him with a wave.

He looked up at the iron gate in the east wall—ajar, just as promised. Beyond it, trimmed hedges, flagstones, and the sprawling manor where DeMarco was likely watching and waiting.

"Let's go to work," Salvatore whispered.

The east gate led to a narrow stone path lined with trees and sculpted marble busts. At its end, a small utility door sat half open, the light above it flickering intermittently.

Two of Salvatore's men swept forward first—Rico and Matteo's cousin, Bruno. They checked the corners, then waved the rest through.

Claudia slipped in next, leading five others. Salvatore followed, his revolver heavy on his hip, his heartbeat steady.

The utility corridor was tight and humid, lined with old fuse boxes and the faint hum of maintenance equipment.

Claudia gestured left. "We go this way. West staircase leads up to the solarium. Frankie's team meets us in the garden."

Estate Interior – Upstairs Study Hall

Inside the mansion, Nico paced behind a thick oak desk, staring at the ledger DeMarco had left behind. His pistol lay beside a half-empty glass of bourbon.

"They're in," he muttered.

Matteo stood near the drapes, peering out between the folds. "Like ghosts. No sound. Just silence."

"They don't want him gone quietly," Nico said. "They want

the city to hear it."

"Then we give them a fight they won't forget."

Matteo walked to the hallway, grabbed a bell from the wall hook, and rang it twice—sharp, metallic chimes that echoed down the halls.

It was the old signal: prepare for intrusion.

Solarium Corridor

Salvatore's team reached the base of the stairs. Claudia held a hand up. "Two guards above. I hear them."

She signaled to Rico, who quietly unshouldered his rifle and set up behind the far wall.

The moment the first guard stepped down into view, Rico fired—a single suppressed shot to the throat. The second man turned, stunned, before Claudia rushed forward and took him down with a knife.

Salvatore nodded. "Move."

They climbed the stairs two at a time, slipping through the glass doors of the solarium into the east wing.

South Garden

Frankie's team moved in tandem, cutting through low hedges and past a dried fountain. They encountered a three-man patrol. The firefight was brief and brutal.

One of Frankie's men sprinted back toward the meeting point and scrawled a chalk mark on the corner of the path— confirmation of position.

East Wing Hallway

Salvatore paused at the double doors of the study.

"He's in there," Claudia whispered.

He looked back at his crew. Five men. Calm. Loyal.

"Everyone knows what to do?"

Affirmative nods.

Salvatore took a breath.

"Then let's finish it."

Part II - Interior – East Wing Hallway

The hallway seemed to stretch forever, shadows slanting across polished wood and ornate wallpaper. Salvatore moved with purpose, Claudia and the others just behind. He paused only long enough to check each corner, each open door. Every breath felt carved from glass.

They passed a pair of shattered windows—one still dripping with blood. Claudia glanced toward it. "Frankie's team made it to the west wall."

"Keep moving," Salvatore said.

From behind a doorway, a gun barked.

One of Salvatore's men dropped, clutching his shoulder. Claudia fired three times into the room, and the threat fell silent.

They didn't stop.

Upstairs – Study Hall

Nico DeMarco gripped the pistol tightly, eyes darting between the heavy oak doors and the fireplace behind him. Matteo was calm, but tense.

"They've breached the second floor," Matteo said.

Nico swallowed. "Then they're coming here."

Matteo loaded a shotgun. "We make them bleed."

Outside the door, muffled footsteps crept closer. Nico raised the pistol, aiming it at the entrance. His breath quickened. He stepped toward the hallway—too fast.

The door burst open before he reached it.

Rico stepped through first, his rifle swinging up. Claudia followed.

Nico fired wildly, striking nothing. Salvatore was already inside by the time the second shot rang out.

"Down!" Claudia shouted.

Nico turned, desperate to reach the window. He didn't make it. A bullet struck his spine mid-step, and he collapsed.

Salvatore stood over him, breathing heavily.

"You picked the wrong side," Salvatore said.

Nico coughed once. Then again. His eyes wide, glazed. Then still.

Elsewhere – West Garden

Frankie's crew held their position beneath the arbor, exchanging fire with a squad of DeMarco's remaining loyalists. The air was thick with gunpowder and barked commands.

"Push them left!" Frankie shouted. "Drive them to the east

wing!"

One of his men hurled a Molotov into a hedged corner, flushing two shooters who had been waiting in ambush.

As the fire spread, DeMarco's men faltered.

The house was no longer a sanctuary.

Interior – Second Floor Landing

With Nico down, Salvatore paused in the corridor. The rest of his crew fanned out, clearing rooms. Claudia reloaded, breathing hard.

"He wasn't ready," she said quietly.

"They never are," Salvatore muttered. "He died for a man who wouldn't do the same for him."

From the end of the hall, a door creaked.

Matteo.

He didn't run.

Salvatore raised his pistol. "Put it down."

Matteo stared for a moment, then let the shotgun drop. "I'm done," he said. "It's over."

"Tell him we're coming," Salvatore said. "Tell DeMarco I'm bringing hell through the front door."

Matteo nodded once and disappeared into the shadows.

Part III - Interior - DeMarco's Private Study

Vincent DeMarco stood alone at the window, his hand resting on the frame, watching the garden burn in the distance. The smoke curled upward into the morning sky. Distant gunshots crackled like thunder, but he no longer flinched.

On his desk lay a pistol, untouched, and beside it a half-finished letter. The ink had dried mid-word.

Footsteps echoed down the hall.

DeMarco didn't turn around. "Matteo?"

There was no answer.

The door swung open.

Salvatore entered slowly, his revolver drawn, Claudia and Frankie behind him. They stepped over broken glass, splintered wood, and the blood of men who'd stood for the wrong empire.

"So," DeMarco said without turning. "You made it."

"I said I would."

DeMarco turned, slowly. He looked tired. Older. The king in winter.

"Do you know what you're about to do?" he asked. "What it means to end me?"

"I know exactly what it means," Salvatore said. "It means the last shadow leaves the room."

DeMarco smirked. "You think that makes you free? No chains, no debts, no knives left behind curtains?"

"No," Salvatore said. "But it means my son doesn't have to grow up looking over his shoulder. Not because of you."

DeMarco stepped away from the window. "Then do it. But know this—someone always comes next."

"I'm counting on it," Salvatore said. "That's why I'll be

watching."

DeMarco reached for the pistol on the desk.

He didn't get there.

Salvatore shot him once in the chest. DeMarco stumbled back against the window frame.

A second shot—clean, decisive.

DeMarco slid to the floor.

Silence.

Claudia looked to Salvatore. "It's done."

"No," he said. "Now it begins."

The smoke still lingered as Salvatore emerged from the house. Frankie was beside him, blood staining his coat. Claudia lit a cigarette with shaking fingers.

The survivors of their crews stood in the yard, bruised, bloodied, but standing.

Salvatore surveyed the grounds. Bodies littered the hedges. The mansion's windows were blackened. But it was over.

One of the lieutenants approached. "What now, Don Vitali?"

Salvatore looked toward the rising sun.

"We bury our dead. Then we rebuild."

He walked down the stone steps as the wind picked up.

A new era had begun.

26

The Weight of Kings

Part I - Spring, 1931 - Brooklyn, Vitali Compound

Spring returned to New York with hesitant warmth, the air still laced with the memory of winter's final gasp. At the new Vitali compound, the garden had been built—roses planted where ashes once lay, marble statues glistening, clean of smoke. Eden, Salvatore's once-hidden club and wartime headquarters, now functioned again as a center of power, though far quieter.

Salvatore stood beneath a sycamore tree in the inner courtyard, hands clasped behind his back. He wore no jacket, only a tailored vest and rolled sleeves. His shoulders were square, his eyes alert. No gray touched his hair—he remained a man in his prime.

Across the courtyard, Joseph, just a small boy, ran in circles, chasing a red ball through the trimmed grass. His laughter broke the quiet, a sound more healing than any peace treaty.

Rosa approached quietly, a small smile playing at her lips.

"You're brooding again," she said.

"I'm watching," Salvatore corrected.

She tilted her head. "Same thing with you."

He didn't argue. Joseph tumbled and rolled, then got back up giggling.

"He's innocent of all of it," Salvatore said. "He won't stay that way forever."

"That's the world's doing," Rosa replied. "Not yours."

Salvatore looked at her. "It has to hold, Rosa. Or it all comes back."

Claudia sat across from Frankie at the Eden, a stack of ledgers between them. The room had been reupholstered, the bullet holes patched, the bookshelves full again.

"We lost two shipments last month," she said. "But we gained two new fronts in Queens. Lombardi's staying quiet. Navarra too. No signs of ambition."

Frankie grunted. "Not ambition we can see."

Claudia closed the ledger. "Salvatore doesn't want a new war."

"He never does," Frankie replied. "But peace is just war waiting in line."

They both looked up as Salvatore entered.

"We're stable," Claudia said quickly.

"Then let's stay that way," Salvatore said. He didn't sit. "Call a meeting. I want every captain, every earner, every face who calls this family home."

Frankie raised a brow. "Something wrong?"

"No," Salvatore said. "But we've come out the other side of fire. And they need to hear it from me—what we are now. And what we'll never be again."

The Eden Grand Hall was filled with whispers and smoke. Dozens of chairs lined the tiled floor. Old soldiers. New blood. Accountants. Street runners. Friends and former enemies. All seated, all waiting.

When Salvatore entered, the room stood.

He made no speech from a podium, no gesture for silence. He simply stepped to the center and waited. Quiet returned like a tide.

"You all know what we've done," he said. "What we've buried. What we've won."

He let the pause hang.

"We are not shadows anymore. We are not dogs to be turned on each other by silver-tongued traitors. We are not the past."

He looked around.

"If you want war, you'll find it elsewhere. If you want to bleed for power, you're in the wrong house. But if you want to build—brick by brick, name by name—then you stay."

Another pause.

"This family is not ruled by fear. It is held together by loyalty. Earned. Not bought. Never bought."

He nodded once.

"Tomorrow, we begin again."

And with that, he left.

No applause. No cheers. Only the hum of men remembering they had survived.

Part II - Spring, 1931 - Manhattan, Lombardi Penthouse

The view from the 17th floor of the Hotel Manhattan was cloudless that morning, the skyline stretching out like a field of steel blades. Marco Lombardi stood in a dark blue robe, sipping a neat glass of scotch. Behind him, the polished parlor gleamed, every surface clean, every light dimmed to golden warmth. A gramophone played a soft jazz tune.

His consigliere, Emilio Parelli, read from a ledger in a velvet armchair.

"Shipments from Havana are ahead of schedule. No resistance from any of the Vitali fronts. Navarra hasn't moved since the sit-down in January. And DeMarco's territory—well, it's gone. Absorbed piece by piece."

Marco smiled faintly.

"DeMarco never understood the long game. Too busy demanding tribute, barking orders, stomping around like a butcher in a crown. Now he's rotting in a grave Salvatore dug with his own pride."

Emilio looked up. "Vitali's become stronger. Tighter. He's earning loyalty. Respect."

Marco didn't disagree. He stepped to the sideboard, dropped a single cube of ice into his glass, and topped it off. "Respect is a currency. Like fear. You lend it to a man, he spends it on illusions. Let Salvatore think he's emperor. Let him polish his marble and plant his roses."

He turned toward the window again, watching a line of smoke curl into the air from the Brooklyn industrial corridor.

"I pushed Navarra into silence. Fed DeMarco false confidence. Pulled Salvatore into war knowing he'd win—but not without bleeding. And now?"

He raised his glass slightly in salute to the city.

"Now the tables are quiet, and the streets are mine."

Emilio closed the ledger. "You played them all."

"I guided them," Marco said. "When you whisper into the wind long enough, the storm starts repeating your words."

He sipped his scotch, savoring the silence.

"They believe the war is over," he said. "They believe peace came at the tip of a bullet."

He walked toward the painting above the fireplace—an oil rendering of Augustus Caesar surrounded by soldiers, all heads bowed.

"Let Salvatore raise his son in the garden," Marco said. "Let him think he controls the strings."

He turned back to Emilio, his eyes cold and steady.

"I am the puppeteer."

Part III - Spring, 1931 - Brooklyn, Vitali Compound, Dusk

The sun dipped low, casting long shadows across the courtyard. Lanterns had been lit early, their flickering light dancing over the worn stone pathways and glinting off the bronze statue near the garden's edge—a lion, regal and poised.

Salvatore stood beside it, hands in his pockets, watching Joseph chase fireflies in the grass. Rosa sat nearby on a bench, embroidering in the fading light, humming softly.

There was peace here, honest and hard-won. And for the first time in years, it felt like it might last.

Claudia approached from the archway, her boots quiet against the stone.

"They're gone," she said. "All the captains. Every one of them pledged. Quietly. Without question."

Salvatore nodded. "Good."

"They believe in this future. In you."

"They believe in what we've survived. That's different."

She stepped closer, watching Joseph for a moment. "What about him? Do you still want this for him?"

Salvatore's gaze lingered on his son. "Yes. He'll inherit more than land and title. He'll inherit something stronger—stability, legacy, respect. Not just from fear, but from order."

Claudia tilted her head. "He's still a child."

"And that's why we build now," Salvatore said. "So when he's ready, he'll take the crown without ever needing to draw a blade."

Claudia nodded and left without another word.

Salvatore's study was quiet save for the ticking of the grandfather clock in the corner. Frankie entered and closed the door behind him.

"Lombardi hasn't moved. Navarra's gone dark again. The rest of the city's holding its breath."

Salvatore poured two fingers of whiskey and offered one to Frankie. "Let them hold it a little longer."

"You think it'll last?"

"No."

Frankie raised an eyebrow.

"But it doesn't have to," Salvatore said. "It just has to be long enough."

"For what?"

Salvatore looked to the window, to the stars just beginning to show. "For Joseph to be ready. For him to take what I've built and carry it forward. Stronger. Smarter."

They drank in silence.

Joseph had fallen asleep hours earlier. Rosa carried him to bed, kissed his forehead, and left his door open just a crack.

Salvatore stood on the balcony alone, the city sprawling before him in lights and darkness.

Below him lay kingdoms built on blood. Alliances spun like silk. Enemies quiet—for now.

He closed his eyes.

Tomorrow would come. And it would bring whatever it brought.

But tonight, the lion rested.